"I want to help you save the diner."

Braden watched as Piper's beautiful brown eyes widened with surprise. The shock on her face made him want to laugh out loud, but he knew the situation was far from humorous. The Snowy Owl diner was at stake, and although he'd agreed to provide his assistance, he wasn't sure if he even believed it could be saved.

"A-are you serious?" she asked, sputtering. She was shocked he'd changed his mind so quickly. Last night he'd been so firm regarding his decision not to help her out with the diner.

"Completely," he said, a smile twitching at the corners of his lips. "Whatever you need is what I'll do."

She pressed a hand to her chest. "You will? Really? You were so decisive last night. What made you change your mind?"

Braden paused before answering. "Because I owe you, Piper."

"For what?" she ⬚⬚⬚⬚⬚⬚⬚⬚⬚⬚⬚ m her eyes.

Telling her the tr⬚⬚⬚⬚⬚⬚⬚⬚ wouldn't want to⬚⬚⬚⬚⬚⬚⬚ be indebted to he⬚

Belle Calhoune grew up in a small town in Massachusetts. Married to her college sweetheart, she is raising two lovely daughters in Connecticut. A dog lover, she has one mini poodle and a black Lab. Writing for the Love Inspired line is a dream come true. Working at home in her pajamas is one of the best perks of the job. Belle enjoys summers in Cape Cod, traveling and reading.

Visit the Author Profile page at Harlequin.com.

Alaskan Christmas Redemption

Belle Calhoune

LOVE INSPIRED
INSPIRATIONAL ROMANCE

If you purchased this book without a cover you should be aware that this book is stolen property. It was reported as "unsold and destroyed" to the publisher, and neither the author nor the publisher has received any payment for this "stripped book."

LOVE INSPIRED®
INSPIRATIONAL ROMANCE

Recycling programs for this product may not exist in your area.

ISBN-13: 978-1-335-48845-9

Alaskan Christmas Redemption

Copyright © 2020 by Sandra Calhoune

All rights reserved. No part of this book may be used or reproduced in any manner whatsoever without written permission except in the case of brief quotations embodied in critical articles and reviews.

This is a work of fiction. Names, characters, places and incidents are either the product of the author's imagination or are used fictitiously. Any resemblance to actual persons, living or dead, businesses, companies, events or locales is entirely coincidental.

This edition published by arrangement with Harlequin Books S.A.

For questions and comments about the quality of this book, please contact us at CustomerService@Harlequin.com.

Love Inspired
22 Adelaide St. West, 40th Floor
Toronto, Ontario M5H 4E3, Canada
www.Harlequin.com

Printed in U.S.A.

Peace I leave with you, my peace I give unto you: not as the world giveth, give I unto you. Let not your heart be troubled, neither let it be afraid.
—*John* 14:27

To my husband, Randy. Thanks for being
my best friend. Forever and always.

Acknowledgments

I want to thank all of the readers who have so
enthusiastically embraced Owl Creek, Alaska.

A special thank you to my editor,
Emily Rodmell, senior editor Melissa Endlich
and the entire Love Inspired team
for working so hard to make the line shine.

Chapter One

Piper Miller placed a Closed sign on the front door of the diner and locked up. She let out a heavy sigh as she rested her back against the frame and pressed her eyes shut. "No rest for the weary," she muttered as she stood up straight and began walking around the place, making sure it was tidy for the morning rush. She'd been going full speed since 5:00 a.m. with no end in sight.

All she wanted to do at the moment was to head home and crawl under the covers where it was nice and warm. Sleep was the only time she ever got a break from all her troubles. Being the owner of the Snowy Owl Diner meant she bore the full responsibility of the establishment's success or failure. At the moment there really wasn't anything to cheer about. The restaurant was knee-deep in financial trouble, and it wouldn't be much longer until she would be forced to close its doors. Everyone in her hometown would be disappointed in her.

It was a crushing feeling to know how badly she'd messed up her dad's legacy.

She looked up and met her father's gaze in the black-and-white photo she'd lovingly hung above the cash register. With his dark brown skin, wavy hair and dimples, Jack Miller had been a charismatic and unforgettable man. To her he'd been Papa. Father, friend, boss. She couldn't quite escape the shame she felt in having failed to turn things around at the diner she'd solely inherited. After conducting a thorough review of the books, she'd discovered the diner had been bleeding money for quite some time. Shockingly, her father had kept it to himself.

If something drastic didn't happen soon to increase revenue, she would have to close the place or sell it. Harboring this secret was stressful. She had confided in her best friend, Rachel Lawson, and her sister-in-law, Sage Crawford, about the financial strain she was under, but neither knew the severity. Both women had promised to keep her situation in confidence at her request. She wasn't sure it had been fair to hold Sage to the vow now that she was married to her older brother, Hank.

Even though Piper was single, she knew married couples ought not to keep things from one another. Sadly, her father had kept everything hush-hush, not even confiding in his own wife. She didn't have the heart to tell her mother or Hank the truth about the diner's finances. The loyalty she felt toward her father prevented her from doing so. She didn't want either of them to think less of him. Jack Miller had been such a proud, hardworking man. It seemed almost inconceivable he'd been struggling for years to keep the diner afloat. At the moment everything appeared to be bleak. Hopelessness wasn't an emotion she had ever imagined experiencing during Christmas. This holiday season might prove to be the worst of her entire life. If she lost ownership of the diner, it would be a catastrophic blow, one she might never recover from.

Piper walked toward the kitchen and began collecting the trash to put out back. Normally it was her employee Jorge Vega's job to do so, but with a pregnant wife ready to deliver their first child, Piper had sent him home hours ago. She felt a pang in her heart at the realization that she might have to let Jorge go if things at the diner didn't improve. That would break both of their hearts. He was such an outstanding employee and an even better human being.

She pushed the back door open and lugged the plastic bag outside, then deposited it in the large metal container. The scent of pine and peppermint hung in the air. Every time she stepped outside it smelled like impending snow. Although the blessed holiday was weeks away, everyone was full of expectation. All the storefronts in town were gaily decorated with mini Christmas trees, tinsel and presents.

How she wished that she could be excited about the most sacred and wonderful time of the year. In Christmases past, Piper's head had been filled with snowmen and sleigh bells, Christmas carols and nativity scenes. She wasn't sure if she could even celebrate this year with so much hanging over her head.

A sudden noise startled her, and she jumped as a dark figure appeared in the glow of the back door light. Who on earth would be lurking out here at night?

"Braden!" She raised a hand to her chest and let out a relieved sigh at the familiar sight of the brown-haired, green-eyed man. Although his hair had grown a bit too long and he looked like he hadn't shaved in days, he still looked like her Braden North.

Well, he hadn't exactly been *her* Braden for quite some time.

"Hey, Piper. I hope it's not too late to stop by." He shoved his hands in his pockets and rocked back on his booted heels. His hunter green parka—his favorite color—almost matched his extraordinary eye color. With his winter hat and jeans, he looked rugged and masculine. He was a welcome sight, considering how rarely she laid eyes on him.

"For you? It's never a bad time," she said lamely, trying not to sound awkward.

On impulse she threw herself against his chest and wrapped her arms around him. No matter what had gone wrong in their friendship, Braden was still her best friend. They had been besties since preschool. She felt his body tense up before he broke away from her, then watched as he took a step backward. Hurt washed over her. It pained her deeply to have such a rift between herself and someone she cared so much about.

"Come on inside," she said, beckoning him to enter through the back door. Braden followed behind her, reaching for the door and holding it open as she walked through it.

Once they were inside, Piper flipped the lights back on above the booths. Now that Braden was here, she wouldn't be leaving for a bit. She had something pretty heavy to discuss with him—her predicament regarding the diner. Truthfully, she wasn't feeling very confident about sharing her troubles with him, considering the fact that he hadn't been interacting with her in any meaningful way in a very long time.

There was a reason she had reached out to him a few days ago. Hadn't she always been able to lean on him when she was afraid or troubled? After her father's death, Braden had been a rock, until he'd abruptly left town to chase danger all over the world as an adventure junkie. It still didn't make sense to her. Braden had always loved Owl Creek, Alaska. He'd said time and again there was no finer place to live. But then he'd disappeared and stayed gone for the last three and a half years. It had broken her heart to lose her best friend. And even though he was back in Owl Creek, he still didn't feel present. Things between them were tense.

It was all so strange, especially when she had no idea what she'd done to make him so cold and aloof toward her. Perhaps their friendship had just run its course and Braden didn't have the heart to tell her. Instead, he'd been giving her the brush-off for years.

"I got your message. Sorry it's taken me so long to get over here," he said, sounding sheepish.

"It's all right. I know you must be getting readjusted to life here in town, not to mention spending time with Sage."

Recently, Sage Crawford, now her sister-in-law, had arrived in Owl Creek harboring a huge secret. She had been stolen at three months old from Braden's family, the Norths. After Sage had recently been reunited with the North family, Braden had returned to Alaska to celebrate the good news and to connect with his long-lost sister. Although he'd been back in town for weeks after being gone for such an extended period of time, he hadn't done a single thing to reconnect with Piper.

"So, what's up? It sounded pretty important." He wasn't quite looking her in the eye, she realized. He seemed fidgety. She stuffed down the hurt. It was important to focus on the matter at hand—telling Braden about her predicament with the diner.

"Why don't we sit? I've been on my feet all day." Being a restaurant owner meant she was in a constant whirl of motion, which took a toll on her legs and feet.

Braden nodded and went toward the nearest booth. She sat down across from him, letting out a sigh of relief. She watched as he removed his hat, then ran his hand through his shoulder-length hair. It looked good on him in a way most men couldn't get away with. But he'd always been easy on the eyes, the guy most likely for all the other girls in their class to have a crush on.

For Piper, he'd always been more than a good-looking guy. He'd been home, her soft place to fall. She would give almost anything to go back to those carefree days when they had been able to finish each other's sentences.

"I'll cut to the chase," she said, locking eyes with him. "I wanted to ask for your help. It's about the diner." Although she was trying to keep her composure, her voice cracked. "It's in big trouble, Braden. If I don't do something very soon, I'm going to have to close the Snowy Owl."

Braden North wasn't sure he quite understood what Piper was telling him. The expression stamped on her face was one of intensity. And panic. With her tawny-colored skin and wide-set eyes, Piper was adorable. Most would say beautiful, but it was hard for him to think of her in those terms. For so long now, she'd been his closest friend. Until he'd ruined everything.

He prayed he was misunderstanding the situation with the diner. It meant everything to her. And her family. Not to mention the residents of Owl Creek.

He knit his brows together. "Close it? Are you saying the diner is at risk of shutting down?"

His gut tightened at the look of utter devastation on her face. "Yes, that's exactly what I'm saying." She choked back tears. "The diner is in bad shape financially, and I—I'm afraid there's no way to rein it back in before the bottom falls out."

"Piper. Slow down. What happened?"

She bit her lip, appearing overwhelmed. "Things started out fine with the diner, and then I did a thorough review of the books. What I discovered was pretty shocking. Daddy had been struggling financially with the diner before he passed away, but he never told anyone. After I uncovered all of the financial difficulties, all of these problems started to happen at the diner. There was a leak in the roof, and I had to get it fixed and close the place for two weeks. That meant two weeks of lost revenue in addition to the cost of the roof repair. Because of a loophole in the insurance, I had to pay for it myself. Then there was a problem with the stoves and the hot water tank. Things just started spiraling out of control, and pretty soon the place was bleeding money with all the repairs."

Piper stopped talking, and he had the impression she wanted him to weigh in on the situation. The information coming out of Piper's mouth was mind-blowing. Jack had always been responsible and prudent. The news was shocking, considering she'd inherited the establishment with no mortgage. It had been hers lock, stock and barrel. But the Snowy Owl being in a precarious financial state changed everything.

He opened his mouth, then closed it. Braden needed to be mindful of Piper's feelings. If he expressed his disbelief, she might look even more miserable than she already did. And he couldn't do that. He'd already done enough to shatter her world.

"I know what you're thinking, Braden. How did all this happen? Trust me, I've asked myself that question a million times." She let out a ragged sigh. "I wanted so badly to carry on Daddy's legacy, so I thought I could fix everything that was wrong. I've been trying to turn things around for years, all while making sure Hank and Mama didn't find out."

He chewed his lip. "Piper, are you sure things are so dire?"

She shook her head. "There's no way the diner can survive for very much longer. From what I was able to glean from the books, it's been a slow, steady decline. Our revenue has been down, and we can't quite seem to bounce back. Our customers are exploring other options.

"A few restaurants opened up on Main Street so there's more competition than ever. Plus I have employees to pay. I haven't even taken much of a salary for myself over the past few years. The money just hasn't been coming in."

"So, are you considering telling Trudy or Hank what's going on?"

Piper's mother—Trudy Miller—owned a popular bed-and-breakfast in Owl Creek. Warm and lovable, the innkeeper and Piper were very close. Hank was town sheriff and Braden's own brother-in-law after his marriage to Sage. Even though Braden was trying to distance himself from Piper, all roads seemed to lead back to her.

"I haven't told them anything," she admitted ruefully. "Before you tell me I should have, just hear me out. Hank has been through so much, and when this whole thing started he was raising Addie as a single father. And my mother is trying to make ends meet at the inn. There's been a big drop-off in guests, so she's been really worried about her own business. Plus she's still reeling from losing my dad. She puts on this facade of everything being all right in her world, but she's still grieving the loss."

"It must've been tough all this time dealing with it yourself," Braden said, sympathy rising up inside him for the situation she'd been placed in all this time.

"I did confide in Sage and Rachel, although I've asked them both to keep it confidential. The last thing I need is for the entire town to find out." She let out an agonizing sob. He wanted to reach out and hug her, but he resisted the impulse.

"I'm so sorry, Piper. I can certainly inquire about withdrawing some money from my trust fund to help you out. I've been dipping into it to fund my travel and living expenses for the last few years, but there's still a sizeable amount left." Although he'd come home to Owl Creek to meet his sister, Sage, he had also come to the realization that he needed a job to pay the bills. He couldn't travel the world forever seeking adventures. His folks had made it pretty clear that he couldn't go on like this, and they wouldn't be funding his travels if he ran out of his trust fund money.

"That's not why I asked you here, although I appreciate your offer. I couldn't take money from you, especially since there's no way of knowing if a cash infusion would be sufficient. I have to figure out a way to increase business, something I can sustain over time." She smiled at him. "It's nice to know we're still friends."

"Of course we are," he said, sounding unconvincing to his own ears. They both knew things had drastically changed between them, but he was the only one who knew why. He hated this awkward feeling between them. He would give anything to enjoy the ease of their former friendship. A memory of them gliding down Chinook Hill on their sleds flashed before his eyes. Braden wondered if they would ever get back to that place in time when such things were normal.

"I wanted to ask you to work with me to come up with a way out of this mess." The words tumbled out of her mouth.

Work with her? Oh no. He couldn't allow himself to spend prolonged periods of time with Piper. It was too risky. He might blurt out the truth and lose her forever. He didn't trust himself not to slip up and tell her everything.

"Piper, I'm not the right person to help in this situation."

"Why not? I think you're the perfect one to help me out. More than anyone else I've ever known, you have a way of seeing the big picture and finding solutions to problems. If the two of us put our heads together and brainstorm, maybe we can find a solution. Perhaps I won't lose the diner after all."

His heart was breaking at the pleading tone in her voice. Piper couldn't mask her desperation if she tried. It was stamped all over her face. He reached across the table and gripped her hand. "I'm sorry. I wish there was something tangible I could do, but at this point, you need an expert to step in, someone who can steer you in the right direction."

"But why can't that be you? You're one of the smartest people I know. I trust you, Braden."

"You shouldn't!" he blurted out.

Her immediate reaction was to look crestfallen. Her beautiful brown eyes filled with tears. He let out a groan. Tears were his weakness. Even when they'd been little kids Braden had hated the sight of his best friend crying. It had always reached inside him and tugged at the most tender part of his heart.

"Please don't be upset. It's just that a lot has changed over the past few years."

She wiped away tears with the back of her hand. "So much so that you can't help out an old friend?" she asked in a low voice. "At one point in the not so distant past we were best friends, Braden. We finished each other's sentences. We promised we'd always be there for each other, come what may. I'm asking for you to help me."

There was no point in stringing her along. He just needed to let her know he wasn't the one who could help out. "I don't think I can, Piper," he said.

Disbelief flared in her eyes along with a flash

of pain. He steeled himself against it, knowing he couldn't act on pure emotion. He clenched his teeth and willed himself to stay strong.

Silence stretched between them until Piper jumped to her feet.

"Don't let me keep you!" She ground out the words. Her cheeks were flushed and there was a dangerous glint in her eyes. He'd seen that look before on a few occasions, and he knew what it meant. Piper tended to wear her emotions on her sleeve. It was one of the things he loved most about her. She radiated authenticity.

He didn't want her to hate him. "It's not that I don't care. I just—"

"You just can't. Is that it? I think it's time for you to go. I need to close up the place." A mutinous expression appeared on her face.

How could he explain his reluctance to be around her without confessing everything to her? She might be upset with him, but at least she wouldn't despise him.

He walked to the doorway and turned back to face her. "I'll be rooting for you. I know you probably won't understand this, but I need to get my own life in order before I help anyone else." Piper didn't betray a single emotion upon hearing his words.

Braden walked out of the diner and into the cold Alaskan evening. He heard the click of Piper locking the door behind him, and it left him feeling empty inside. More than anything in the world he wanted to help her find a way to hold on to the diner. But he knew spending time in her presence was too dangerous. He was keeping secrets from her, and if they spent time together, he didn't trust himself not to crack under the pressure.

Give me strength Lord, he prayed. *I'm going to need it.*

Braden couldn't remember a time when Piper hadn't been his best friend. She had nestled her way into his heart with her plucky attitude and willingness to be adventurous. Even as kids she'd always been the one to take up his dares and plunge headfirst into the abyss. Whether it was sled-dog racing or riding in a hot air balloon, she'd always been up for a challenge. He'd never imagined her not being a huge part of his life.

Everything had changed four years ago when her father was killed in a snowmobile accident. Braden tried not to remember that afternoon, but the memory of it kept crashing over him in unrelenting waves. He'd been hanging out with some former high school buddies—Tim Carroll, Andy Summers and Lou Warren—on a lazy Saturday afternoon when they'd decided to go snowmobile riding. Usually they raced each other through the trails and then back to the starting point. Braden was known in Owl Creek for his love of extreme sports and adventures. He was the most skilled rider among all of them, and he loved being up on the mountain with the arctic wind whipping through him as he zipped along the trails.

Braden had been surprised to see Jack Miller on the trail that afternoon. It wasn't very often Piper's father took time off from the diner for recreational activities. When Jack had pulled Braden aside and asked to speak to him in private, he'd been upbeat about it, thinking the older man wanted to discuss a surprise event for Piper's upcoming birthday. Much to his surprise, Jack had been stern and full of censure.

Jack's harsh expression had spoken volumes. "I've been hearing stories about you and your friends speeding down these trails, Braden. Considering what happened last year to Mac Crenshaw, I advise you to slow down and take the proper precautions. This town doesn't need another tragedy and neither do your parents."

Braden had bristled at Jack's tone and his reference to Mac's death, as well as his family's tragic loss of his sister who was kidnapped as a baby. Mac had died overseas in the service and the entire town had mourned the death of the hometown war hero. Losing Mac had affected all of Owl Creek. He'd felt embarrassed that his friends had been within earshot of Jack's comments. He hadn't appreciated being spoken to as if he was an unruly child. Sometimes his family treated him the same way since he'd been the youngest member of the North family in Lily's absence. "I'm always careful, Jack," he'd said as anger coursed through him. "So are my friends. We know these trails like the back of our hands."

"People here in town are talking about riders driving irresponsibly down these paths. It's a safety issue!"

"So you're just assuming it's me who's breaking the rules, right? I can ride these trails blindfolded. I've never been in a single accident." His voice had been raised and full of unbridled anger.

Although Braden and Jack had always gotten along, the tension hanging in the air between them had been palpable. It was the first time they'd ever been at odds. Jack's chin trembled as he responded. "Pride goeth before a fall, young man. You still have a lot of growing up to do." With a shake of his head, Jack had walked away.

Looking back, it had all happened so fast. One moment Jack had been standing beside him and the very next moment he'd sped off down the mountain trail on his snowmobile. Although Braden had been concerned about his jerky movements, he hadn't followed behind him. About an hour later their paths had crossed when Braden spotted Jack riding the trail up ahead of him. He'd made a mental note to smooth things over between them later on. A short while later, he'd been the first person to come upon the crash scene, witnessing a mangled snowmobile smashed into a grove of trees. Braden had instantly recognized Jack's bright red snowsuit. He'd jumped off his snowmobile and raced toward Jack, who had been ejected from the vehicle. He'd performed CPR until help arrived, all the while praying for Jack. He hadn't known until the next morning that Piper's father hadn't survived his injuries. His guilt had been overwhelming. He'd agitated Jack prior to the crash.

If they hadn't argued, perhaps he never would have crashed.

The worst part was that everyone had praised Braden for administering medical assistance to Jack and staying at the scene to help in any way he could. He'd kept quiet about his quarrel with Jack, not disclosing to a single soul how upset Piper's father had been with him prior to the accident. For the past four years, he'd been stuffing down his feelings of guilt, unable to forgive himself or come clean about it. He'd never seriously considered telling Piper the truth.

There wasn't a single doubt in his mind that if Piper knew he'd played a role in her father's death she wouldn't want anything to do with him. Not now or ever.

Chapter Two

Braden looked out the huge bay window of the North family home and admired the snowcapped mountains looming in the distance. They were majestic and beautiful. Although Owl Peak was much smaller than Mount Everest—the last mountain he'd climbed—this vista represented home to him. He took a big swig of his coffee and let out a beleaguered sigh.

Last night had been rough. He couldn't quite get Piper's face out of his mind. The expression of hurt and disappointment on her face gnawed at him. He hated letting her down so badly. They had never had such a huge strain between them in their entire lives.

He didn't know why he'd even ventured over to the Snowy Owl Diner last night in the first place. It had been a colossal mistake.

No, that wasn't true. He did know why he'd made the trip over there. He missed Piper. Not seeing her on a regular basis for the past three and a half years felt like torture. There wasn't much he didn't miss about her—the hearty laugh, her curly mane of hair and the corny jokes she always had at the ready. She was one of the best people he'd ever known.

He had traveled the world in pursuit of adventures, all the while trying to avoid talking to Piper or having to look her in the eye. But he hadn't been able to snuff out the memory of her. It had been impossible not to miss their weekly movie dates or sharing chocolate cherry milkshakes with her at the diner. He didn't have anyone to read comic books with or go ice-skating with on the town green. There was no one in the world who could replace Piper.

She was one of a kind and as unique as an individual snowflake.

How could he have said no to Piper in her time of need? She was in this predicament because she'd been given ownership of Jack's business well before she'd been ready to run the place all on her own. Although she'd worked at the diner for many years as a waitress, she clearly hadn't been made aware of any problems with the business. And the Snowy Owl hadn't been financially stable when she'd assumed ownership. Although Piper was smart, she'd been placed in a situation over her head. He felt like a selfish jerk in turning her down, but he didn't know any other way to handle the situation. Spending time around Piper while withholding the truth about his argument with Jack would be impossible.

But had his decision been the right one? He kept going back and forth, second-guessing himself. It hurt him to realize she was struggling with this issue all by herself since she hadn't told her mother or brother.

Helping Piper was the right thing to do, especially since he carried the weight of her father's death each and every day of his life. It was the reason he'd been running away from Owl Creek for such a long time. It was why he couldn't bear to be in Piper's presence for very long. How could he look into her doe brown eyes and not make a full confession?

He was a coward, plain and simple. Piper and her family deserved the truth, yet he couldn't give it to them. Always in the back of his mind was his responsibility to his own family. His parents had been put through pure torment for twenty-five years after his sister, Sage, had been abducted as an infant from their home in Owl Creek. She had only recently been reunited with the family after decades of separation. A confession from him about being responsible for Jack Miller's death would subject them to even more pain and scrutiny. The thought of telling Piper the truth rattled him. So far he'd convinced himself it wouldn't be the right move. It was far better that she viewed him as being self-absorbed or disinterested rather than the person who had caused her father's death.

"So, how's it going?"

He turned from the window to see his sister coming down the stairs.

"Are you enjoying being back in town?" Sage asked. "You've been gone a long time."

Braden grinned. His newfound sister always made

him smile. Her presence in their lives was a dream come true. Sage was always cheerful and sunny. She was wise beyond her years. Considering all she'd been through, it was downright awe-inspiring. Most people would be bitter about being raised by the woman who'd kidnapped her, but Sage's faith had allowed her to handle the situation with grace and an abundance of courage.

"It's going fine. I'm having fun getting caught up on all the town gossip," he said, a teasing tone in his voice. "Of course your return was the talk of the town. In a good way of course."

She flashed him a grin. "It was an interesting way to come to Owl Creek. That's for sure."

"But it all ended well, didn't it? You and Hank found each other, and our family became complete with you in it. It was an answer to years of prayers."

Sage nodded in agreement. His sister seemed very content with her life. She was a wife, stepmother and teacher. Braden couldn't help but envy her.

"I may be overstepping, Braden, especially since we're still getting acquainted—"

"You're my sister, Sage. You can ask me anything." He smiled. "Well, almost anything."

"Hank told me so much about your friendship with Piper, but since you've been back I haven't seen the two of you together at all. Matter of fact, Piper mentioned to me last week that you hadn't even been over to the diner. Did you two have a falling out?"

"No. Not at all," he said, feeling slightly uncomfortable talking about Piper. He shouldn't be surprised in a town as small as Owl Creek that people had noticed their estrangement. Even though she was fairly new to the community, Sage had become fast friends with Piper. And now they were family too—sisters-in-law.

"She could use a friend right about now," Sage said.

"Are you talking about the diner?" Piper had told him she'd confided in Sage, so he wouldn't be telling her anything she didn't already know.

Sage's cheeks reddened. "I don't want to talk out of turn. I promised not to say a word."

"It's all right. I went by the diner last night, and Piper told me everything." He shook his head. "I still can't believe she could lose the Snowy Owl. It's her pride and joy, not to mention it's a direct link to her father. They were very close."

She bit her lip. "I wish she would tell Hank. I'm not sure how much longer I can keep quiet. We're family now, and it doesn't feel right not to share this with my husband."

"I understand your dilemma, but I think Piper is afraid of disappointing her family. You didn't know Jack, but he lived and breathed that diner. It was everything to him." Braden felt himself getting choked up. Piper's dad had been a hero in his eyes—a former vet who had proudly fought for his country, then settled down in Alaska and met the love of his life in Trudy, who'd been widowed a few years earlier. Trudy might find it hard to understand why Jack hadn't told her his business was struggling. It might come as a bit of a shock.

"Hank loves her. And so do I. She's my sister-in-law. Even if we can't afford to help her monetarily, surely he can assist her with trying to get the diner back on track."

Braden shrugged. "Shame can hold people back from asking for assistance. I think she's afraid of being judged." He knew it from his own personal experience. It was a powerful emotion. It had been weighing on him for years.

"I'm glad she confided in you, as well. I think the more she talks about it, the less weight will be on her shoulders," Sage said with a nod. He appreciated his sister's perspective. She was proving to be a compassionate and wise woman.

"I agree. She wanted me to work with her to figure it all out, but I didn't think it was a good idea. She needs an expert. There's really not anything I can do."

Sage appeared crestfallen. "Braden! You have to help her. You'll never forgive yourself if she loses the Snowy Owl and you didn't step in during her time of need."

"We're not as tight as we used to be," he explained. "It just wouldn't work."

Sage narrowed her gaze as she looked at him. "I know there's a story in there somewhere, but I'm not going to push you to explain what's going on between the two of you when you clearly don't want to share it with me." Sage pointedly raised an eyebrow.

Braden held up his hands. "Wait a minute! It's nothing like that. We've only ever been friends."

"Well, if that's true, then you should have no problem at least giving her a shoulder to lean on. She needs you, Braden." Sage's eyes were full of sincerity. With her dark hair and heart-shaped face, it was uncanny how much she looked like their mother, Willa. She radiated the same air of confidence.

She needs you.

Sage's words served as a dose of reality. He had shut down a bit over the past few years. It was a defense mechanism born out of his desire not to feel anything. In the aftermath of Jack's tragic death, Braden had felt everything acutely. In the end it had driven him away from Owl Creek, his family and Piper. The time away had left him homesick and without his bearings. As much as he'd tried to deny it, home was a healing balm for him.

Perhaps he should have just told the truth from the beginning. At least he wouldn't be walking around feeling like he was going through the motions. Denying Piper his help would be heaping more pain onto her plate. She was already hurting pretty badly. Because of his confrontation with Jack, the good-hearted diner owner had crashed his snowmobile and died. Piper had lost her father, a loss she would never get over. Hank and Trudy had suffered, as well. Didn't he owe Piper something? The least he could do was help her out of this awful mess. Maybe despite what he'd done he could make her life better. Perhaps he could ease her suffering and help her find a solution.

Maybe he could manage to do the right thing, which was what he should have done four years ago. For so long Braden had been running away from his culpability. Perhaps by assisting Piper he could find a way to make things better for her.

The next morning a group of local bird-watchers managed to bring a smile to Piper's face. Although there were still many vacant seats at the diner, the Snow Birds gathered at the Snowy Owl a few times a week to enjoy breakfast before they set out on their bird-watching adventures. Seeing such loyal customers frequent the diner caused a small amount of hope to blossom inside her. Despite all the goodwill flowing in the air from the group, she still felt hurt at Braden's refusal of her request for help.

Perhaps she had always looked at him with rose-colored glasses, but for their entire lives it had always been Braden who'd rushed to her defense, whether from childhood slights or the times she'd been singled out for being brown skinned with a white mother. He had never failed her. She couldn't understand why he refused to help her now. What had she done to push him away? She'd racked her brain on countless occasions, always coming up empty. Perhaps he had simply outgrown her. The very thought of it made her chest tighten.

She lay in bed at night asking herself that niggling question, along with a bigger one.

Why had God forsaken her? She had been praying for relief from this nightmare for months. As a
woman of faith she had a hard time dealing with the
concept of God hearing her prayers but not answering them. Her mother was fond of saying God didn't
always answer your prayers in the way you imagined He would, but He still listened. Piper hoped
He continued to listen to her. She needed Him more
than ever.

And still she was no closer to a solution than before. Time was ticking away with Christmas right
around the corner. She let out a sigh. Piper hadn't
even decorated the diner with the usual holiday trimmings. Tears pricked at her eyes as she scanned the
place. As a child, one of her favorite things had been
to come to the diner at Christmastime so she could
help her parents put up the tree and decorate the front
windows. There had been ornaments and tinsel and
holly. The Snowy Owl had always overflowed with
holiday cheer!

Her parents had always made a romantic show
of kissing under the mistletoe. While Hank had
groaned, she'd loved every moment of it. Knowing
her parents were a true love match had been her foundation in a sometimes shaky world. Although she
loved her hometown and its residents, being biracial
hadn't always been easy. There had always been a
few people here and there who hadn't been accepting of her parents' union or of her. At times it had
threatened to break her spirit. But having Hank as an

older brother and Braden as a best friend had been the best protection of all from ignorant mindsets.

"Good morning, everyone!" Beulah North, matriarch of the North family, came bustling through the doors of the diner with greetings rolling off her tongue. Dressed in her signature pearls and a navy blue cape-style coat, she carried herself with an elegance that Piper admired. She looked down at her own pink-and-white uniform with her name boldly etched in black above her heart. Piper wouldn't be winning any fashion contests anytime soon. Most days she barely looked at herself in the mirror or did much to her hair other than wash and go or pull it up in a simple ponytail. As it was, she barely wore lip balm.

Perhaps she could get some pointers from the grande dame of Owl Creek. Piper had to smile at the trendy pair of Lovely boots Beulah was wearing as she strode toward the counter. There was something almost regal about the woman.

"Hey, Beulah. You're looking stunning today. What's the special occasion?" she asked in a teasing voice, knowing her friend dressed this way each and every day.

"No occasion, my dear. I just like to look nice for Jennings," she said, referencing her husband. "You know we're going to be celebrating our sixtieth wedding anniversary soon."

Piper grinned. "That's wonderful. You two are definitely something to aspire to."

"Thank you, my dear. What a wonderful compliment," Beulah said, beaming. "I was wondering if you'd like to partner with North Star Chocolates this year for the annual Christmas walkabout. We can do chocolates and pizza or something along those lines. It's such a lovely way to ring in the holiday and thank all of our customers for being so loyal."

Piper had almost forgotten about the local tradition in Owl Creek where most of the local businesses got together to spread holiday cheer. All of the townsfolk walked throughout the downtown area and were able to sample goodies, win prizes and walk away with gift bags filled with holiday loot. During the event, all of Main Street was lit up with festive lights in celebration of Christmas. Ever since she was a child, Piper had enjoyed this special town activity. And the Snowy Owl had always participated, with her dad dressed up as Santa and handing out toys to every kid in town.

She hated to commit to Beulah when so much uncertainty was circulating around her business. But how could she say no to the kindhearted matriarch? It was tradition. "It sounds good, Beulah, although I might toy around with the pizza this year. I've been trying to add things to the menu. I might offer a reindeer pizza."

"Smart thinking, young lady," she said, patting Piper on the shoulder. "From what I can see, you've done a great job of making this place your own. Jack is a hard act to follow. I've never seen a man with such a zest for life." She let out a sigh. "I still can't believe he's not here with us."

Although she wanted to experience nothing but joy when her father's name was mentioned, Piper still felt so much angst. The loss seemed so fresh. And unresolved. Unanswered questions still lingered. What had caused him to veer off the trail and crash? He had always been such a careful driver, and there hadn't been a lot of ice on the trails that particular day. It still baffled her.

People always talked about moving on and the stages of grief, but for Piper it felt as if no time at all had gone by. The last four years were just a blur and it seemed almost like yesterday when Jack had been here with them, spreading his warmth and kindness throughout Owl Creek.

"Thanks, Beulah. It's time for me to take some risks with the menu so people don't get bored with the fare. Also, I can't make too many changes, or I could alienate the regulars." It was such a fine balance, Piper realized. In order to increase business, she needed to jazz up the place and offer something different, but what would happen if the regular customers didn't like the alterations? In the past few years she'd slashed prices, reworked the entire menu and hosted karaoke nights. Nothing had worked to increase the diner's profit. She admired her father so much for running the diner so successfully for such a long time even though he'd faced some financial challenges in the last few years.

"No risks, no reward," Beulah said pointedly. "Now, if you could package up a few slices of the gooseberry pie, I would be mighty obliged. It's a favorite of Jennings and mine." She winked at Piper. "With my sweet tooth, I consider myself an expert. So keep them coming."

"Aww. That's nice of you to say. I wish I had time just to bake pies." She warmed at the compliment regarding her baking. It was a hobby for her, and over time she'd discovered her pies were a crowd favorite at the diner. Although she loved coming up with new recipes, she simply didn't have the luxury of doing it on a regular basis. And she couldn't afford to take her eyes off the prize right now. She needed to focus on the diner itself and trying to save the family business before the bottom fell out.

Piper busied herself packaging up the gooseberry pie slices for Beulah. All of a sudden the sounds of her favorite holiday tune—Nat King Cole's "The Christmas Song"—came blasting from the jukebox. It was a sentimental song for her because her father had also loved it. When she glanced over toward the jukebox, she saw Braden standing there gazing across the diner at her. She felt a pang in her heart at the sight of him. What was he doing here? He was the last person she'd expected to see after last night's uncomfortable conversation.

She handed the pie box to Beulah and watched as Braden made his way over toward them. Her hands felt moist at the sight of him. Since when had his presence made her nervous? Would they ever get back to that place in time when everything had been pure ease between them?

"Fancy meeting you here," Beulah said as Braden

leaned down to place a kiss on his grandmother's temple. "I'm not sure if it's possible, but you seem even more handsome than when you left town."

Braden chuckled. It brightened his features and drew attention to his straight white teeth and strong jawline. It was nice to see him so lighthearted. Lately he'd been way too serious. Some might even call it somber. "Grandma, you're way too kind," he drawled.

"I speak the truth. Now that I have my pie, I'm going to run. I'll see you two later," Beulah said, giving a little wave before walking away with a spring in her step.

"What brings you here?" Piper asked Braden, trying to sound casual. He didn't need to know she was still fuming about last night. She was doing her very best to play it off.

"Can we talk for a moment? In private?" he asked, shifting from one foot to the other.

Piper nodded and gestured toward the kitchen. She really didn't want anyone to overhear them talking. People here in town spread gossip like wildfire. She wouldn't be at all surprised if the townsfolk were already buzzing about their fractured friendship. Folks in small towns tended to notice huge shifts in relationships.

He followed behind her as she swung the door open and walked toward the back office. Once they were both inside, she turned toward Braden so they were facing each other.

She folded her arms across her chest. Although

she was tempted to tap her foot on the hardwood floor, she resisted the impulse, knowing it would be rude. Instead, she counted to ten in her head before speaking. "What did you want to talk about? I really don't have much time for chitchat. We're really busy this morning."

"I noticed you have a nice crowd out there. That's good, huh?"

"It's decent, but it comes in dribs and drabs," she said with a shrug. "The diner needs consistent revenue." It was going to take something drastic and life-altering to save the Snowy Owl. She could no longer put her head in the sand and hope for brighter days. She needed to take action.

"I wanted to swing by and make sure things were all right between us," he said, meeting her gaze head-on. "It's never a good thing when you're angry with me."

"I think we both know things have been strained between us for a while. Last night just proved I wasn't imagining things," Piper said in a matter-of-fact tone.

He moved closer toward her, swallowing up the space between them. "I know it might sound like a cliché, but it's me, not you. I've just been so mixed up lately. I didn't say it well last night, but I've been floundering a bit. Being away from Owl Creek for so long left me a bit rudderless."

After last night Piper hadn't believed she could feel sorry for Braden, but hearing him talk about being lost made her ache for him. She could tell he was trying to stay strong, but there was a hint of sadness emanating from his eyes. Before things went downhill between them, she would have known exactly what was going on with him. Now, she didn't really have a clue.

Perhaps it had been selfish of her to ask such a huge favor of Braden without knowing what was going on with him.

"I'm sorry about that," she said. "Maybe being back home will get you back on track."

"That's what my mother said." He made a face. "She also told me I need to get my life in order rather than trekking around the world seeking out adventures."

"You had a good run. It had to end sometime." It was pretty mind-boggling to her that he'd traveled to so many places and done so many incredible things. A part of her admired him while another part couldn't imagine being away from the quaint Alaskan town she loved so much.

"Well, I'll probably end up taking a position at the family business. One of the perks is being supplied with all the chocolate I can eat." Although his tone was light, Piper could detect a note of resignation in his voice. At one point Braden had thought about a career in law, but it hadn't worked out the way the North family had planned. He'd never made it to law school. Braden had decided he wasn't cut out to be an esquire.

The North Star Chocolate Company was the North family's business. There was a chocolate factory and a shop in Owl Creek. It was a big tourist attraction as well as a staple for everyone in town. Run by Braden's parents, Willa and Nate, and his grandmother, it was a huge financial boon for the town. As chief executive officer, Beulah wanted all of her family members to be a part of the business. Although she knew Braden loved his family, both of them knew he wasn't cut out for a desk job or working for the chocolate corporation. The great outdoors was the perfect working environment for Braden. He was in his element when he was hiking or mountain climbing or dog mushing.

"Are you sure that's what you want?" she asked. Even though Braden had refused to help her, she still wanted him to be happy. She honestly couldn't picture him being his authentic self while working at the family's business.

He looked away from her. "We don't always get what we want, but I love my family and I know being away for the last few years has been hard on them. With Sage home, it's the first time in over two decades that my parents have had all three of their children in one place. That's pretty special for all of the Norths."

"I know it is. And I'm happy for all of you." She frowned at him. "Is that what you wanted to talk about?"

"No, that's not it," he answered with a shake of his head. "I came here to tell you that I want to be there for you, Piper. Our friendship means the world to me. I want to help you save the diner."

Chapter Three

Braden watched as Piper's eyes widened with surprise. The shock on her face made him want to laugh out loud, but he knew the situation was far from humorous. The Snowy Owl Diner was at stake, and although he'd agreed to provide his assistance, he wasn't sure if Piper even believed it could be saved. From this point forward, she would have to tell him everything about her situation. He would have to look over the books with a fine-tooth comb. If he was truly going to help her, he needed to understand exactly what she was facing. The good, the bad and the ugly.

"A-are you serious?" she asked, sputtering.

"Completely," he said, a smile twitching at the corners of his mouth. "Whatever you need is what I'll do."

She pressed a hand to her chest. "You will? Really? You were so decisive last night. What made you change your mind?"

Braden paused before answering. "Because I owe you, Piper."

"For what?" she asked, confusion radiating from her eyes.

Telling her the truth wasn't an option. She wouldn't want to know why he would forever be indebted to her. "For a million different things. You've always being in my corner. How could I say no to you when you've always said yes to me? No matter what trouble I got into or the problems I laid at your feet, you always jumped in to help me. There's no way I could do any less for you."

Tears slid down Piper's face, and she made no attempt to wipe them away. She bowed her head, and he could see her lips moving. When she raised her head back up, Braden saw pure happiness emanating from her eyes.

"Thank you, Braden. I'm so grateful that you changed your mind. I know it's complicated, but in my heart I truly feel that I was meant to carry on Daddy's legacy. I just can't imagine my life without this place in it. I'm willing to do just about anything to save it."

Braden couldn't envision Piper losing ownership of the restaurant either. It would be agonizing for her. Not to mention Trudy and Hank. They were all invested in it. The townsfolk would be both saddened and upset. Piper would be the subject of endless gossip about the circumstances of her losing ownership of the Snowy Owl. She wouldn't be able to bear it if the townsfolk discovered that the diner had been struggling since before her father's death.

He knew Jack's reputation was important to Piper. People would sympathize with her as well, but he knew she would be inconsolable. If there was even a small chance of them reversing things, he wanted to give it his all. It would be his penance for shaving years off Jack's life. If it hadn't been for him, Jack might be here today, doing everything he could to boost the restaurant and spreading his effortless charm throughout the establishment.

"We should meet up so you can give me an opportunity to look over the books and all of your monthly bills along with revenue. That'll at least give me a snapshot of what's been going on."

Piper made a sad face. "Sure thing. I hope you see something in there that I missed, but I crunched the numbers over and over again. It's not looking good."

"We have to look at all your options. You might need a lawyer or a consultant."

She shook her head. "I don't have money for an attorney. It's a lack of money that's gotten me into this situation in the first place." Piper let out a frustrated groan.

"Why don't we meet this evening to try and sort some of this out?" he suggested. From what he'd initially gathered, they had only a short window of time to get things dealt with before everything imploded. That needed to be prevented at all costs.

"That sounds good. Come by after I close up," she told him. "I have to get back out there, but I'm so thrilled you changed your mind about helping me." She flashed him a smile. "In case you didn't realize it, I'm super grateful."

"Get back to work," he said, making a shooing motion with his hands. "I'll see you tonight."

After Piper rushed out of the office, Braden sank down into one of the chairs and let out a ragged breath. *Fake it until you make it.* He usually hated the expression, but at the moment it held a deep significance. He had managed to put on an award-winning performance with Piper. Hopefully she hadn't detected anything lurking under the surface. She was a fairly intuitive person, and she knew him so well. He never wanted her to see the cracks.

It was hard keeping secrets from Piper, especially one as substantial as this one. Although he had spoken the truth about owing her, there was so very much he'd omitted—truths he was too scared to ever confess to her.

And so instead he would help her figure out where she stood with her long-term ownership of the diner, and if possible, help her hold on to it. Maybe then he wouldn't feel as if he owed Piper a debt he could never repay.

The rest of the day passed by in a blur for Piper. Although she still felt nervous and scared about the future, just knowing Braden would be assisting her in the weeks ahead made her feel as if she wasn't so alone. It was a comforting feeling. Piper was tempted on a daily basis to confess everything to her mother and Hank, but she always stopped short before she did so. Telling them the disastrous news about the diner would change the way they regarded Jack, and she couldn't bear the thought of them feeling such a deep sense of disappointment in her father.

If she could turn things around and rescue the establishment, no one would ever have to find out that the diner had been struggling well before she inherited it. Braden's surprise appearance at the diner had lifted her spirits and given her a hearty dose of hope. Some might call her foolish for being so optimistic, but the alternative was too horrific to imagine. Having it ripped away from her would serve as a gut-wrenching blow. Failure really wasn't an option.

But now she wasn't handling this situation by herself. Braden was by her side.

For the first time in ages, she'd felt as if she had been looking at her best friend instead of the cold, remote stranger he'd transformed into. But even though Braden was saying all the right things, something still seemed off between them. If they were going to work together to save the diner, she needed to figure out what had changed so dramatically between them. She knew she wasn't imagining things.

It had started in the aftermath of her father's death. Although Braden had been a rock for her to lean on, he had exhibited signs of strain and discomfort. It was as if he didn't feel right in his skin all of a sudden. Had she leaned on him too much? Was he uncomfortable because he hadn't been able to save Jack's life with his CPR techniques? Although she'd tried to convey to Braden how grateful she was for his lifesaving attempts, maybe it hadn't sunk in. Perhaps he couldn't move past not being able to save her father's life.

Midafternoon Hank stopped by for lunch with his best friends, Gabriel Lawson and Connor North, Sage and Braden's brother. Friends since they were toddlers, the three men always referred to themselves as the Three Amigos. Just watching the camaraderie flowing so naturally between them caused a sharp pang to shoot through her. It used to be like that with her and Braden. They had been inseparable. Everything had been effortless.

Look on the bright side, she reminded herself. *Being in such close proximity to Braden could change things*. Perhaps they just needed to get back to their natural rhythms. Maybe then their friendship would return to being what it once had been—spectacular and full of ease. That and saving the Snowy Owl was all she truly wanted for Christmas.

"Hey, little sis. How's it going?" Hank asked as he approached her, a smile gracing his handsome face. There were few people in her life who she flat out adored. Hank was one of them. As town sheriff, he was a beloved figure in Owl Creek. With his sandy-colored hair and blue eyes, her older brother looked nothing like her. But regardless of their physical differences, they were still bonded by blood and their love for one another. Like her mother always said, *Real love is color blind*.

"I'm doing all right," she answered, matching Hank's grin with one of her own. "Today has been fairly busy. Considering how up and down things have been lately, it's a blessing."

Hank seemed to be studying her. He was gazing at her intently as if trying to read her facial expressions. "So, how's the bottom line? I know running a restaurant isn't easy, especially in a small town like Owl Creek. You must have taken a hit with the new establishments that have opened down the street."

She waved her hand around, highlighting the restaurant. "We're keeping our heads above water," she answered. "The customers keep coming back, so it's all good, Hank." It pained her to tell half-truths, but she didn't know what else to do at the moment.

Now would be the time to tell her brother all about the diner's precarious financial situation and the very real possibility that she would have to close the Snowy Owl's doors. He would be shocked, and he might even lecture her about withholding the truth for so long. But at least this huge secret wouldn't be weighing on her conscience. Maybe then she would be able to breathe normally without feeling a sharp pain in her chest. She knew something else with a deep certainty. Hank would move mountains to help her, which was the exact reason she couldn't confide in him. Her older brother was a loyal and compassionate man who had been through a lot over the past few years. Now, after his marriage to Sage, he had finally found happiness. There was no way she could place this huge albatross around his neck, regardless of what it might cost her.

"That's good to hear, Piper. Don't be a stranger. You and Mama need to come over for dinner real soon."

Piper cocked her head to the side. "Did you learn to cook in the last few months? Because the last time you made a meal for us you almost burnt your house down."

He reached out and playfully tweaked her nose. "You're a regular comedian aren't you? Sage has been teaching me some of her recipes." He puffed out his chest. "I made pot roast the other night."

Piper fanned her face. "As I live and breathe. Love has sure transformed you, Hank Crawford."

"It surely has, and I couldn't be any happier about it," he said, brushing away curls from her temple then placing a kiss there. "I have to head back to the sheriff's office, but I'd like to see you sometime away from the diner." He shook a scolding finger at her. "Remember, if you live, eat and breathe this place, it'll lead to burnout." With a warning look, he strode away from her toward the door.

Burnout. Little did Hank know how close she was to being consumed by the flames. She needed something good to happen to turn things around. She needed God to show her that the dream her father had nurtured for so long wasn't going to turn into ash. Piper pressed her eyes closed and prayed. *Dear Lord, please hear my prayer. I need Your help more than I ever have before. I'm in trouble and I'm scared of what's to come. Please help me weather this storm.*

During her break, Piper dug around in the office and located all of the files and paperwork she wanted to share with Braden. Right before closing, he arrived and sat down in their usual booth, the one they had always chosen throughout their childhood. Once she closed up the diner, she joined Braden at the table and without saying a word slid the file toward him. She nervously nibbled at her nails as he read through the papers. After he'd looked through the files and spreadsheets, Braden sat back in the leather booth seat and frowned.

Piper leaned across the table. "So? Don't leave me hanging. What's the verdict?"

Braden let out a low whistle. "I'm not trying to make you feel bad, but I can't tell you more than you already know—the diner has been in trouble for a while now. Your father was putting money into it to try and get traction, but those efforts never paid off for any sustained period of time." He shook his head. "I don't know if he had a strategy to improve things, but the struggles continued until his death."

Her heart sank. Had she really been so foolish as to think Braden would instantly find an answer to her terrible predicament? She fought against the feeling of despair threatening to pull her under. She was trying to stay positive, but it was becoming more difficult with each passing day.

"Maybe I should just throw in the towel," she said, her lips quivering with emotion. "It isn't fair to blindside Hank or Mama. If I lose the diner, it's only right to give them fair warning."

"Piper, I'm trying to be straight with you, but I also don't want you to give up hope."

Piper crossed her hands in front of her in prayer-like fashion. "Do you really think there's a way out of this?"

"I do. It's the most wonderful time of the year. If ever there was a time to have faith, it's during Christmas." Braden drummed his fingers on the table. "Remember when a chocolate cherry shake would make everything feel better? I miss those days." His voice sounded wistful.

Leave it to Braden to mention their favorite sweet treat and lighten the mood. Her father had come up with his own special recipe for the drink, and it became a customer favorite. There had even been a name for it on the menu. The chocolate cherry bomb shake. Piper and Braden had made it their go-to drink whenever they'd headed over to the diner for an after-school treat. There had been nothing quite like it on the Snowy Owl menu. She hadn't continued making them after her father's death, but now she was wondering if that had been a mistake.

"Do you want me to make us some?" Piper asked, her stomach grumbling at the idea of the delectable treat. She'd been so busy this evening she hadn't even stopped to eat a bite of dinner.

Braden nodded vigorously. "I'll never say no to the cherry bomb."

Piper busied herself in the kitchen making the shakes for the two of them, leaving Braden to look over the information she'd provided. When she brought the treats to the table, Piper relished the look of absolute delight on Braden's face as he took his first sip. He closed his eyes and let out a sound of utter contentment.

"In a perfect world, you'd be able to make a million dollars off this recipe," Braden said, taking another lengthy sip. "You could go on one of those food shows and blow everyone away with this concoction."

"I wish. Then my problems would be solved," she murmured, knowing such a thing was impossible. But it was nice to dream, wasn't it? She and Braden had shared so many hopes and wishes over the years. Some had come true while others were pie-in-the-sky fantasies. She wondered if he would still share those precious dreams with her or whether it was just another piece of their relationship that had been altered by time and space. She was hoping that spending more time together would repair all the fractures in their relationship. It was hard to imagine a future without Braden in it.

He quickly finished his drink with a satisfied sigh.

"Good to the last drop, huh?" she asked, chuckling at his empty glass.

"It would be a pity to waste any of it," he answered, grinning back at her.

This felt nice, Piper thought. Despite the dire circumstances, she was enjoying a bit of the old camaraderie between them. It meant the world to her.

"Hey. I need to run outside for a moment. I forgot something in my car," Braden said, jumping up from his seat. Before Piper could respond, he was halfway out the door.

A few minutes later there was a banging sound.

When she walked over, she could see Braden standing there with a huge Christmas tree tucked under one arm. She wrenched the door open and stepped aside as Braden traipsed in. For a moment he battled to get it past the doorway. With a huge grunt, he pulled it across the threshold. He leaned the tree against the wall as he stopped to catch his breath.

"This is what you forgot? A ginormous pine tree?" she asked, feeling stunned by Braden's sweet gesture. She had been so preoccupied by her troubles that she hadn't even thought to do anything to make the diner look festive in anticipation of the holidays.

"It was a surprise," he said. "I couldn't run the risk of you saying no."

"I would never say no to a Christmas tree," Piper said as she inhaled the fragrant aroma of pine. "It reminds me too much of hearth and home. It's funny how a smell can transport you all the way back to childhood when all you wanted for Christmas was to find a bike under the tree or the latest Barbie dollhouse."

Braden made a face. "I remember you forcing me to play with that dollhouse and then getting mad when I wouldn't play by the rules."

"That's because you wanted the dolls to do karate moves when they were supposed to be in a fashion show." Piper laughed at the sweet trip down memory lane. They truly had been in each other's pockets all through their childhood. He had always been her soft place to fall. She hoped he always would be.

After a little bit of wrangling, they managed to drag the tree over to a spot by the window. Braden raced back outside and returned with a tree stand. He held it up triumphantly and placed it in a strategic spot by the tree. Piper stood on one side while Braden placed the tree in the stand, then asked Piper to hold it steady while he tightened the screws at the base. When it was secure, they both stepped back to admire the tree in all its glory. It was beautiful and majestic, reaching all the way to the ceiling. There was even a little space at the top for the star. Once it was all decked out, the customers would love it. Now all they had to do was add water to the base to keep it fresh and hydrated.

Piper swallowed past the huge lump in her throat. She couldn't help but think about her sweet and lovable father. He'd loved Christmas more than anything, and he had sprinkled his irrepressible brand of holiday charm all over Owl Creek. Because of him, the diner had radiated pure love and warmth. Having the tree here brought a huge piece of her father back to her.

"How did you know exactly what this place needed?" she asked, her throat husky with emotion. "It's simply perfect."

"I remembered how festive it looked in years past. Not to mention if you walk down Main Street all the other businesses are decked out with all the Christmas trimmings. It's that time of the year when all is merry and bright. The Snowy Owl needed a little holiday bling."

"It reminds me of all the Christmases when Daddy would take us to pick out the tree. Once we'd selected the perfect one, he'd tie it to the top of the truck and then bring it back here so we could decorate it." She let out a sob. "I can't tell you how much I miss him. I'd give anything to have him right here with us."

Braden resembled a deer in the headlights. His eyes went wide, and he looked at her without saying a word. He seemed to be completely overwhelmed by her emotion.

Perhaps he too was still trying to wrap his head around the events of that day on the mountain.

"I know I've said it before," she continued, "but my family is mighty grateful for everything you did to try and rescue my dad after the accident. The paramedics said your efforts were nothing short of heroic."

"I—I wish I could have done more. I'm no hero, Piper. Not by a long shot." He spit out the words as if rejecting the notion that he could ever be anybody's champion. "It's getting late. I really should get going. I'll be in touch." His expression was unreadable. He stuffed his arms through the sleeves of his winter parka and jammed his knit hat on his head before making his way outside.

In the blink of an eye, he was gone. The lovely rapport between them had been shattered without warning. One moment he'd been warm and engaged, then he'd shut down on her and run away as if his feet were on fire. His behavior was startling. Every instinct told her that Braden was keeping secrets from her. She should know. He'd been her partner in crime since they were in diapers.

And it terrified her because at this moment he was the only person in her life she was truly counting on to help her out of the terrible mess she found herself in.

Chapter Four

Braden woke up the following morning feeling none of the relief he'd expected to experience for having agreed to help Piper with the Snowy Owl. There was still a weight sitting on his chest. He couldn't help but wonder if it would remain with him for the rest of his life.

Hero! Hearing the word tumble off Piper's lips last night had caused a churning sensation in the pit of his stomach. He'd practically bolted out of the Snowy Owl rather than look Piper in the eye and accept her praise. If one more person referenced him by using the H word, Braden thought he might lose it. He couldn't be any less of a hero if he tried. He wasn't brave or true.

That was the problem with returning to Owl Creek. Everyone thought they knew him, but in reality they didn't have a clue. He wasn't like his older brother, Connor, who did everything right in every situation. Perhaps he should just tell the truth and

spare himself the guilt. Who was he kidding? He'd
spent the last three and a half years running away
from his inability to face his best friend and confess everything to her. Even though their relationship was strained at the moment, Piper was still his
friend. A little pressure had been lifted from his
shoulders the moment he'd agreed to help her turn
the business around.

Jack Miller had been a beloved man in town.
Braden couldn't remember ever hearing a single
person say a bad word about him. Piper had always
enjoyed a wonderful relationship with her dad. In
Braden's opinion she'd put her father up on a pedes-
tal where nothing could touch him. Even now, Piper
seemed to gloss over the fact that the diner had been
experiencing financial problems during her father's
tenure as the owner. She was blaming herself for
not being able to turn things around, when in reality she'd inherited a struggling business.

Braden helped himself to a glass of orange juice
and a gigantic blueberry muffin from a large basket
on the kitchen counter. The large house was quiet. He
felt an immediate sense of guilt at being the only one
still at home when everyone else was at the chocolate factory. Even his grandfather had ventured out
of the house despite his tendency toward being a bit
of a recluse. Braden looked around him, scanning
the gleaming hardwood floors, the porcelain back-
splash behind the counter and the copper pans hanging by the stove.

He knew he'd been raised as a child of privilege

since his family were the owners of a very profitable and well-known chocolate business. Growing up in a quaint, small town in Alaska had been wonderful. But he'd always been aware of the huge gaping hole in his family. Sage's abduction had left unresolved trauma and indelible scars. Although he'd always felt loved, he had been acutely aware of his parents' despair. Throughout his childhood, they'd kept his missing baby sister's nursery intact, like a shrine to her memory. The mere mention of her name, Lily, had always reduced his mother to tears. Over time Braden had learned not to speak her name and to stuff down his heartfelt feelings about his sister. It had taken a toll on him, a fact he'd buried for many years.

Sage's return had done so much good for his family. Being reunited with his sister after twenty-five years had been a life-affirming event.

Braden let out a groan after checking the time on the kitchen wall clock. He was supposed to be at North Star Chocolate's offices in fifteen minutes to meet with his older brother, Connor, about assuming a position in the company. Not wanting to be late, Braden quickly grabbed his wallet and keys before making his way to his truck.

Driving into the heart of downtown Owl Creek was a visual treat for the eyes. He grinned at the sight of his hometown all decked out in the holiday trimmings. It almost made him feel hopeful.

Once he reached the factory, he exited his vehicle and entered the large brick building. The heady aroma of chocolate filled his nostrils as soon as he stepped foot inside. It was a scent that smelled like home to Braden, bringing back warm and cozy memories of childhood. The smell was as familiar to him as his own name. As soon as he could walk, Braden had been a frequent visitor to the chocolate factory. It had been a little bit like a Willy Wonka experience. He and Connor had been extremely fortunate as children to have every confection imaginable at their disposal. Braden grinned at the memory of him and his older brother sneaking into an off-limits area and taste testing a limited-edition batch of marshmallow chocolates. By the time Beulah discovered them, both had been sick to their stomachs from overindulging. It had been a long time till either one of them ate another piece of chocolate.

Braden began walking toward the executive offices. He paused along the way to greet employees who enthusiastically called out to him and gave him hugs and warm greetings. By the time he reached his brother's office, Braden felt buoyed by the goodwill of the staff. Somehow he'd forgotten how generous the residents of Owl Creek could be. Braden had known most of them his entire life and during the period of his self-imposed exile, he'd missed them all a great deal.

He rapped hard on Connor's office door, then pushed his way inside, grinning at the quirky items his brother had used to decorate his work space. A five-foot bubblegum machine was in the corner while a cutout figure of Superman rested behind his desk. Signs of the impending holiday were everywhere—a miniature Christmas tree sat on his desk with the lights twinkling and shimmering; a green-and-red wreath with a big white bow hung on the wall.

Connor's eyes lit up when Braden entered his office. He stood up from his chair and greeted him with a warm clap on the shoulder. "Hey, Braden. It's good to see you here. Thanks for coming by."

Connor, dressed in a crisp pair of khakis and a dark shirt, radiated confidence and an air of laid-back professionalism. With his dark hair and blue eyes, he'd always impressed the ladies in town. A confirmed bachelor, Connor wasn't likely to settle down anytime soon, although his two best friends, Gabriel Lawson and Hank Crawford, had both recently gotten married to the respective loves of their lives. Braden wondered if it would change the dynamic between the Three Amigos since his brother was now the only single one of the trio. Frankly, Braden couldn't imagine Connor falling in love and devoting himself to home and hearth.

"It feels good to be here. It's been a while since I've walked through these doors." A feeling of pride swelled up inside him. What his family had built with their chocolate company was incredible. They had created a great deal of jobs right here in town, along with giving the local economy a big boost.

"We've missed you." Braden heard the raw emotion crackling in his brother's voice. Although Connor was a jokester, there were moments like this where his heart shone like the sun. Braden had always looked up to his suave older brother, and he always would.

"Ditto," he said, his throat feeling clogged with sentiment. He wasn't certain he could put into words how deeply he'd ached to be reunited with his family. He'd missed seeing them on a daily basis and the closeness they all shared. No matter the distance, his family had always been at the center of his heart, right along with Piper. Being away from them had been a self-imposed punishment. He hadn't felt worthy of being hailed as a hero.

"So, are you ready to sit in the corner office and join us as an executive?" Connor asked.

"What were you thinking?" Braden asked as a kernel of discomfort lodged in his chest. He had avoided this discussion for so long, and he needed to know what was expected of him. Although he deeply respected the family business, he still couldn't see himself sitting behind a desk all day like his brother. But how could he tell his family that he wouldn't be content doing the very thing they all enjoyed?

"Well, we'd love for you to start as soon as possible. Everyone's excited about having you on board as a member of the executive team." Connor's smile stretched from ear to ear. He resembled a kid on Christmas morning.

Braden nodded. If he started working right away at North Star Chocolates, how would he find time to help Piper? He'd given her his promise after all, and he didn't intend to let her down. He had been disappointing her for way too long. If he didn't follow through, it would put even further strain on their friendship. "Would you mind if I started after Christmas? I promised Piper I would help her out with the diner, and I don't want to leave her in the lurch."

Connor knit his brows together. "You're helping at the Snowy Owl? How so?"

Braden hesitated. He needed to tread carefully. Piper had confided in him about the diner's financial situation, and he didn't want to violate her trust. As it was, he considered himself on shaky ground with her. "It hasn't been easy for Piper to run the diner all by herself. She's a proud person by nature, so she's been reluctant to ask for help."

"Hank would have helped out in a heartbeat if she'd asked. I don't know a single person in town who wouldn't pitch in if Piper needed it."

"Please don't make a big deal out of it with Hank. I don't want Piper thinking I was spreading her business around town," Braden cautioned, cringing at the idea of being in the doghouse again with his bestie. Things were so much better when she was smiling at him rather than glaring.

Connor narrowed his gaze as he stared at him. "There's nothing seriously wrong with the diner, is there?"

"Just a few growing pains. Piper and I have it all under control," he said smoothly, not wanting to tell an outright lie to his brother. From what he'd seen by perusing the books, things were looking dicey for the Snowy Owl. Time was of the essence if they were going to turn things around. But he couldn't tell his brother any of those details.

"Well, I'm glad that you and Piper are spending time together," Connor said. "I was beginning to wonder if the two of you outgrew each other. You haven't been hanging out with her at all."

Braden stuffed down his irritation at his brother's comment. "She's my best friend, Connor. I hope that never changes."

"Happy to hear it," Connor said, grinning. "I'd like to have you on board at the company after the New Year. That way you can help Piper through the holiday season and then join the ranks here as a junior executive in the marketing department. It will be great having the whole family working together."

Braden nodded. He hoped and prayed things would be looking up for Piper and the diner.

Being back in Owl Creek was where he wanted to be, but he wasn't sure about becoming an executive. Throughout his childhood he'd been the kid who had gazed out of the classroom window and yearned to be outside in the fresh outdoors. Not much had changed since then. He always chafed at being indoors too long.

And he wasn't certain how long he could keep up the pretense with Piper. He was struggling to figure out whether or not to come clean about his argument with Jack and realizing that if he didn't he wasn't living up to the person he wanted to be. He wasn't living his faith in the ways he should. *I have no greater joy than to hear that my children walk in truth*. The passage from John washed over him, serving as a potent reminder of what was at stake. Truth was important, particularly in God's eyes.

So far, being back in Owl Creek was proving to be a lot more complicated than he'd ever imagined. And for the life of him, he wasn't certain if he could stay in Alaska much longer without shattering into a million little pieces.

Piper's gaze wandered outside toward the town green where a group of kids were engaging in an after-school snowball fight. A smile twitched at the corner of her lips. Although she loved the diner, sometimes she felt the urge to head outside and play in the snow just like the children she was watching. It would be nice to be carefree and devoid of adult responsibilities. At least for a little while. Her mind flashed back to lazy afternoons spent skating at the lake or dog mushing on the trails at Gray Owl woods. She'd been so blessed to have an idyllic childhood.

Not everyone was so fortunate. Her mind veered toward Braden. Although the North family was loving and tight-knit, Braden had been scarred by the kidnapping of his sister. Life in the North household had been fraught with tension and grief in the aftermath. It had affected every single member of the family in one way or another. Braden had gone inward, as if protecting himself from the world around him. Although she'd always been one of the few people he'd let in, lately that hadn't been the case. He'd built up a barrier between them that she hadn't been able to tear down.

Granted, Braden had agreed to help her rescue the diner, but he was still keeping her at arm's length. What had come between them? She couldn't stop asking herself that elusive question. She'd probably ponder it over for the rest of her days unless she received answers.

"I'll have a ham and cheese omelet with a cup of the salmon stew." Piper's attention swung back to her customer. She jotted down the order on her notepad and smiled at the elderly gentlemen dressed in reindeer pajama bottoms and a thick red sweater. "Coming right up, Otis," she said, trying to make her voice sound a lot cheerier than she felt. Otis Cummings was one of the diner's most faithful customers. Rain, shine or in the midst of a raging snowstorm, she could depend on Otis to show up at the Snowy Owl for his favorites—omelets, sourdough flapjacks with strawberries and a big bowl of cornmeal maple mush. He always washed it all down with a piping hot cup of apple cider.

"Thank you for serving breakfast in the afternoon, Piper. My wife used to make me this very meal for lunch every time I asked," Otis explained, his voice raspy with emotion. "I sure miss her. The holidays won't be the same without June."

Bless his heart, she thought as she recalled how he'd lost his wife a year ago. He was a sweet man who did his best to spread goodwill despite his own devastating loss. He served as a reminder that her family wasn't the only one who'd lost people they loved. Her close friend, Rachel, had suffered the tragic loss of her father in a plane crash back in high school. Like Piper, she had mourned the tremendous void in her life. Somehow, it helped to realize she wasn't alone in her grief. Others were struggling, as well. The loss of a loved one left an indelible mark.

The sound of the bell jingling alerted Piper to a customer entering the diner. She'd placed the bells above the door to add some holiday cheer to the establishment. Every time she heard it jangle, it made her smile. Little by little it felt like she was getting into the holiday spirit. When she turned toward the entrance, Piper felt a little rush at the sight of Braden walking through the door. At the moment he represented hope. Despite the chasm between them, she still felt as if he was a strong shoulder to lean on when she needed it the most. Braden made a beeline in her direction, his strides full of purpose. He had a lean and rugged physique, one that mirrored his active lifestyle. It wasn't surprising to see several female customers watching him with keen interest.

"Hey there." He greeted her with a smile. "So you're running the place and waiting tables?" Braden asked, letting out a low whistle. "Your work really never ends, does it?"

"I'm just subbing for one of my waitresses, Elena," she explained. "She's come down with some stomach bug."

"Put me to work," Braden said, glancing around

the restaurant. "It'll give me a chance to figure out what's working here and what isn't."

"Sounds good if you're up to it," Piper said. "It would be helpful with the dinner rush coming later on." She made a face. "Not that there's going to be a big crowd, but I'd still appreciate the help."

Braden nodded. "Just tell me what to do, and I'll get right on it."

Piper motioned for Braden to follow along with her as she headed toward the counter and put Otis's order on the order wheel. Along the way she greeted customers by name. It was the beauty of living in a small Alaskan village. Everyone knew each other. And when a stranger visited or relocated, they were welcomed to the town with gratitude. Thanks to North Star Chocolate Company, Owl Creek had a steady stream of tourists.

She took a few minutes to explain things to Braden regarding greeting customers, taking orders and how to put the orders in for the diner's cook, Clara Teague. Braden was a quick study, and she watched from a few feet away as he handled his first customers—a group of friends who were catching a late lunch. Piper stuffed down her annoyance as Braden flashed a pearly smile and used his charm on the women. It shouldn't bother her at all since he was doing her a favor and helping out, but it made her feel territorial about Braden, which was utterly ridiculous. They were close friends and nothing more.

And yet she still didn't like seeing women flirting with him. It caused tension to build up inside her. She clenched her hands at her sides, then forced herself to turn away from the sight of it. Her stomach was all tied up in knots and she had no idea why. Perhaps the stress of the situation with the diner was taking a toll on her.

Piper felt someone tugging at her sleeve. When she looked down, Otis was looking up at her with a grin on his face. "Don't worry, Piper. Braden only has eyes for you."

She felt her stomach dip. "Oh no, Otis. Braden and I are only friends." She felt flustered at the mere suggestion that Braden was interested in her romantically. Or that she had her heart set on him.

Otis knit his brows together. He placed a finger on his chin. "Sorry. My mistake. I thought I sensed something brewing between the two of you." He shrugged. "What do I know? I guess my radar is way off."

Piper felt heat spreading across her face as she walked back toward the kitchen. She didn't know what was wrong with her. Normally she would laugh off a comment like the one Otis had just made. Perhaps the tension she felt every time she was in Braden's orbit was messing with her. He was doing a decent job of pretending as if everything was fine, but she saw something lurking in the depths of his eyes that worried her. Things were not fine between them. She knew it with a deep certainty.

Right after the last customer departed and Piper hung up the Closed sign, Braden slumped into a booth seat. He wiped his hand across his brow. "Wow. I really worked for that paycheck."

Piper sat down across from him. "Ha. I see you've got jokes. I can't afford to pay you, but I will supply you with as many chocolate cherry shakes and bowls of fish chowder you desire. Or anything else you'd like from the kitchen."

Braden began sniffing the air around him. "How about some of that pie you just took out of the oven? It smells incredible."

"Sure thing. Let me go see if it's cooled down." Piper headed into the kitchen where two pies were cooling. One was a blueberry rhubarb, the other a pecan. Piper felt the temperatures with the back of her hand. She cut two pieces of the blueberry rhubarb pie, then grabbed a carafe of milk from the fridge and poured two tall glasses. After placing everything on a tray, she walked back to the table, doing a careful balancing act. Braden jumped up as soon as he saw her, saying, "Do you need help?"

"I've got this," she said, placing the tray on the table. "I grew up in this diner. I've been balancing trays since I was a kid. And I've gotten a lot better at it."

As soon as Piper sat back down, they both dug into the pie. It always felt gratifying when someone liked one of her pies. Baking was one of her favorite pastimes, and it had become a source of stress relief for Piper. The fact that customers enjoyed them was an added bonus. Judging by Braden's reaction, he was a fan. It made her feel ten feet tall.

"I've been thinking about next steps," Braden said after swallowing a mouthful of pie. "I found a little intel earlier."

Piper raised an eyebrow. "What exactly does that mean?" She put a forkful of pie in her mouth. The blueberries melted on her tongue, providing a burst of flavor that delighted her taste buds. This particular pie was her favorite, and her customers seemed to be in agreement that it was a winner. It warmed her soul to know her pies were in high demand.

"I staked out the competition," Braden explained. "There are two specific establishments that are your direct competition. Burger Bites and the new pizza joint, Slices. Both restaurants have signature dishes that keep people coming back."

Piper leaned across the table. "Don't tell me… Slices is serving reindeer pizza?"

Braden nodded. Piper let out a groan. "They're also doing make your own pizza nights where customers can create their own signature pizzas. It's pretty popular according to my sources," Braden continued. "And Burger Bites is doing those miniburgers with all the trimmings and serving french fries with gravy and cheese."

"Poutine?" she asked in a high-pitched voice that didn't even sound like herself. "No wonder I'm losing business. They're pulling out all the stops, aren't they?"

"Yep, they sure are," Braden agreed. "I think you should follow suit and feature some one-of-a-kind dishes that will make the diner stand out. Give them something new to look forward to."

She threw her hands in the air. "I thought I was giving the townsfolk what they wanted. Reindeer pizza has always been our thing. My dad used to make it—" She stopped speaking when she saw the look etched on Braden's face. "What?"

"Don't take this the wrong way, but you need to freshen things up a bit. Think about it. It's been four years since Jack ran the place. He probably put reindeer pizza on the menu over ten years ago, right? And even though folks enjoy it, it's not exactly cutting edge anymore."

Piper bristled. "I've kept it as a staple to honor my dad's memory. I'm not taking it off the menu if that's what you're suggesting." The specialty pizza had smoked reindeer, tomatoes, mushrooms, five cheeses and onions.

"That's not what I'm saying. I love reindeer pizza as much as the next guy, but I think you need to switch things up and do something you haven't done before. No risk, no reward."

Piper's heart began beating a crazy rhythm within her chest. Her palms moistened. The notion of doing something drastically different at the Snowy Owl felt terrifying. She'd always made a point to do things in the same vein as her father. Had she been misguided in doing so? Perhaps she'd been so caught up in the past she hadn't been able to see the future. Braden had always given her wise counsel throughout their lives. She knew without question he was coming from a good place. "You have a point, Braden. But I have no idea what to showcase."

"I vote for pie," Braden said, stuffing the remainder of his slice of pie in his mouth.

"Pie?" Had she heard him right? He thought pie was the answer to the Snowy Owl's financial problems?

"Holiday pies with really unique flavors like this one right here," he said, pointing to the crumbs on his plate with his fork. "From what I heard today from customers, they want more pie. You're only making a few pies per week, so a lot of folks never get the chance to purchase it. Increase your production of the pies, and we'll advertise them heavily. And if you really want to go crazy, how about milkshakes?"

Pies? Piper knew the feedback regarding the sweet pastry had been overwhelmingly positive, but she'd never considered them being a draw to attract more steady patrons to the diner. Shakes weren't anything new to the diner since her father had put them on the menu shortly after he opened the Snowy Owl.

"Well, we already have a few shakes on the menu." She frowned. "To be honest, it's not bringing the foot traffic in."

"I don't mean run-of-the-mill milkshakes. These are extreme ones. When I was in Washington State, there was this place that served really unique shakes." He leaned across the table, his features animated. "Think cookies and Twizzlers and cereal adorning the shakes. And edible straws made out of chocolate or graham crackers. You can get really creative, especially since Christmas is coming. I'm thinking peppermint, chocolate and eggnog."

Piper bit her lip. "I'm overextended as it is. I'm not sure how I'll find time to bake all these different pies and create these spectacular milkshakes. Not that I don't like the idea, but I'm short-staffed."

"I'll help you, Piper. I can't bake pies, but I can whip up some shakes that are out of this world. That can be my job. I can also get Connor to promote them at North Star Chocolates and to all the tourists. Trudy can help spread the word at the inn. I know it might seem like a lot, but I think it could really increase sales."

Piper took a deep breath. Things were changing so fast. A part of her felt as if she was being disloyal to her father while another part of her knew her options were limited. In order to save the diner from potential closure, she needed to embrace new things. She needed courage. And even though things weren't back to normal between them, she knew Braden was the right person to be helping her out. He had a wealth of great ideas to help stimulate growth at the Snowy Owl. He was the bravest person she'd ever known—volcano trekking at night in Indonesia, bungee jumping in Australia, skydiving in Africa, along with a host of other adventures. Her best friend wasn't afraid of anything. She wanted to be a little bit more like him.

"I'll have to find someone to help me out with the pies, but if it pays off financially, it will be well worth it." She made a mental note to reach out to a few people here in town who knew how to bake. Perhaps her close friend Rachel might know of some folks. As a nurse, Rachel met with patients in the local community all the time.

"I can put out some feelers, as well," Braden added. "By the way, that tree over there is looking very bare. When do you plan to trim it? This place needs some Christmas bling."

"I want to do something festive with the customers. Perhaps they can help trim the tree or put up some lights. I'm still figuring it out." She let out a sigh. "I guess I'm stalling. Trimming the tree is something my dad loved doing. I can't help but think of him and lament the fact that he's not here with us."

Braden's expression turned somber. "You lost someone hugely important in your life. It's understandable."

Piper nodded. "That's one of the reasons I was so angry with you for leaving town for so long. It felt like a double whammy losing my father and then you." The words practically leaped out of her mouth. For so long now it had been festering inside her, this feeling of being abandoned by Braden. If they were going to move forward with their friendship, it was important to be honest with him. It was scary though. He'd already hurt her once before by leaving her behind. She wasn't sure she was ready to be wounded if Braden walked out of her life again.

Braden looked away from her and began tapping his fingers on the table. It was a nervous gesture he'd been doing for most of his life. A major tell that he was jittery about something. When he opened his mouth to speak, a chill swept through her. She had a very strong feeling that Braden had something important to say. The last time she'd had this hunch he had been announcing his departure from Owl Creek.

"Piper, there's something you need to know," he said in a halting voice. "Honestly, I should have told you this a long time ago, but I—"

A loud rapping sound echoed at the door. It startled both of them and cut Braden off midsentence, leaving Piper to wonder what he had been about to tell her.

Chapter Five

Braden didn't know whether to feel annoyed or relieved when the loud knock sounded at the diner's door. He'd finally summoned the courage to tell Piper the unvarnished truth about the events leading up to Jack's fatal accident when they'd been disturbed. In the blink of an eye, the moment of truth had slipped through his fingers. It annoyed him to no end.

With a sigh, Piper stood up and walked over to the door, peeking through the curtain before wrenching it open. "Mama," he heard her say before Trudy Miller came bustling through the doorway. With her long red hair and colorful hat, she was an attractive, vibrant woman who exuded an air of goodness. Trudy was an eclectic personality in their small Alaskan town. She was a straight shooter who told it like she saw it and treated everyone as if they were an old friend. He watched as Piper enveloped her mother in a tight embrace that showcased their close relationship. Although the two women looked nothing alike, anyone could tell they were related due to their similar mannerisms and the loving way they interacted with each other.

Seeing Piper's mother felt like a kick in the gut. Every time he was in her presence it served as a strong reminder of everything that the Millers had lost. It was hard to look Trudy in the eye and accept all of her kindness and sincerity. Ever since he was a little kid, she'd treated him with such generosity. As Piper's closest friend, there had always been a place for him at the Miller's dinner table.

"Braden! It's great to see you," Trudy said.

"Nice to see you too, Trudy." Braden stood up and greeted Piper's mother with a peck on the cheek. As the owner of one of Owl Creek's most popular inns, she was a beloved figure in town. He hated the awkwardness he felt in her presence, and he wished things could go back to the way they used to be. In losing Jack, she'd lost the love of her life. It was all he could do not to profusely apologize to her for upsetting her husband prior to the crash that ended his life. If only he had the courage to break free from his fear of losing Piper's friendship and disappointing an entire town who believed in him.

"How are things?" Braden asked, trying to ease his discomfort. He was struggling with immense feelings of guilt that threatened to swallow him up whole.

"Pretty good," Trudy answered. "Things have picked up a little bit at the inn with the holidays coming. It seems that everyone wants to visit Owl Creek because of North Star Chocolates and Sage's return to town."

Braden let out a groan. "I wish the media would give it a break. Sage is still trying to settle into her new life with Hank and Addie. She doesn't need to be hounded."

"At least it's dying down a little," Piper added. "Right after the story broke about Sage being the long-lost Lily North, it was sheer pandemonium. Paparazzi were jumping out from behind bushes and taking random photos."

Just the thought of the invasion of his family's privacy made him angry. Where was the compassion for a young woman whose entire life had been turned upside down? His family had been through so much heartache over the years. Why would anyone want to subject them to more scrutiny?

Trudy wagged a finger at him. "On another note, why haven't you come over to the inn to visit me? I've barely seen you at all since you've been back."

"I'm sorry," Braden said. "It's been a bit hectic since I've come home. I wanted to spend some time getting to know my sister and really bond with her. Then there was her wedding to Hank and a bunch of other things that cropped up."

Trudy shook her head. "I still can't believe that Sage came back to Alaska after all the years of loss and separation. God is good! He wouldn't allow secrets to fester in the darkness."

Braden stiffened at the mention of secrets. He

hated thinking that the one he was keeping was as bad as all of the lies Sage's adoptive mother had told her over the years. Those lies had hurt his family and deprived them of Sage for twenty-five years.

"Piper! That tree is amazing!" Trudy said as her gaze veered toward the Christmas tree. "It's just begging to be decked out with ornaments though."

Piper beamed. "It's gorgeous, isn't it? We can thank Braden for it. He brought it in the other night. Now all we have to do is decorate it."

Trudy clapped her hands. "Let's have a tree trimming party. It will be so much fun. I'll be more than happy to help you out with the details. They don't call me Mrs. Christmas for nothing," she said with a chuckle.

"I was thinking of having a party," Piper conceded, "but I want it to be in appreciation of all of the diner's loyal customers and to welcome any new ones."

"Who doesn't love a holiday event? I think it's a great idea," Braden said, nodding his approval. Christmas in Owl Creek was the happiest time of the year without exception.

Braden could see the enthusiasm bubbling up inside Piper. "I think we'd have a nice turnout if we held it the night of the holiday stroll. That way customers can come inside from the cold, get some hot cocoa, sit down for a meal and then help us decorate the tree. And I can figure out a great promo for the pies." She quickly told her mom about Braden's idea to offer more of a pie selection, especially for the season.

"Speaking of pies, I want to order some from you for the inn. My guests are clamoring for some more." Trudy winked at her daughter. "I told them I have an in with the pie maker so it shouldn't be a problem."

Braden saw the look of pleasure etched on Piper's face. He knew it must be gratifying to receive such validation, especially when things were in such turmoil with her business.

"See, Piper? The demand for your pies is increasing every day. You can really spark something if we can figure out how to increase production so they can be a staple at the diner." Braden knew Piper needed to be encouraged in order for her to believe in the potential success of her pies. She wasn't a risk taker by nature, so he wanted to show her what was possible if she stepped out on a limb of faith.

"We? Are you helping Piper with the diner and this pie enterprise?" Trudy asked, turning toward Braden. "If you are, I think it's great. You're one of her closest and most trusted friends." She put her arm around Piper. "This young lady has absorbed a lot of responsibility in the last four years. Sometimes I wonder if we should have stepped in to help out with the running of the place. So much has been placed on her shoulders."

Piper shook her head. "I wouldn't have let you, Mama. You have the inn to run and Hank is town sheriff with a new wife and toddler. From the very start I was eager to carry on Daddy's legacy. That hasn't changed one bit."

"In case I haven't said it lately, your brother and I are very proud of you. I know it hasn't been easy with memories of Jack everywhere in this place." She took a deep breath as she looked around the diner. "It's as if he's in the very air around us."

Braden wanted to say a hundred things or more about Jack, but he felt as if his mouth was filled with cotton. He didn't trust himself to say anything without blurting out the awful truth. Jack Miller had been an upstanding husband and father who had been a huge presence in Owl Creek. Seeing the tears in Piper's eyes caused a groundswell of emotion to rise up inside him. For the first time since Jack's death, Braden's desire to soothe Piper and Trudy seemed more important than his own need to mask his responsibility for the snowmobile accident.

"He is here," Braden said. "In every booth and crevice. He made this place his own. He put his heart and soul as a stamp on the Snowy Owl. I don't think a single person could ever walk through these doors and not remember him." He let out a deep chuckle that emanated from way down in his belly. "I remember how he used to wear those ugly Christmas sweaters every year. He had dozens of them! And each one was uglier than the last."

Piper sniffed back tears. He knew the memory had caught her off guard. His mother had once told him that even when you lost a person you loved, memories of them were everywhere you turned. She'd been referencing his sister, Sage, at the time. Even though baby Lily had been taken from them, the memory of her still remained in their hearts and minds, never to be forgotten.

"You're right, Braden. Although it's particularly painful during the holidays, Daddy's presence is always surrounding us. Some days it feels like a warm, cozy blanket while on others it's just a deep gaping hole." Piper's voice broke, and he watched as she blinked back tears.

"I wish that I could go back to four years ago and tell him not to ride that snowmobile," Trudy said tearfully. Her tone was full of regret. Braden had harbored similar thoughts, always asking himself what if. What if he hadn't argued with Jack before his run? What if he'd apologized and tried to make things right between them? He'd been angry at Jack for accusing him of something he hadn't done, so smoothing things over hadn't been his main priority. Pride had allowed the chance to slip through his fingers.

"He was a grown man who made his own choices," Piper reminded Trudy in a gentle voice. "And like Rachel told me, there's some comfort in the fact that he died doing something he loved."

Rachel had recently married Gabriel Lawson, a local pilot and one of Owl Creek's favorite sons. When she was a teenager, Rachel's father, Lance, had died when the small plane he was piloting crashed. It had only been recently that Rachel had managed to come to terms with the monumental loss. She'd said on many occasions that she would always mourn him, but she wouldn't allow her father to be defined by the manner in which he died. Braden knew how profoundly that knowledge had helped Rachel heal.

Trudy's lips quivered and she inhaled deeply. "Okay, I didn't mean to be a downer. It just hits me sometimes that he isn't here with us. I know that Jack of all people would want us to carry on and enjoy a spectacular holiday season."

"He sure would," Piper agreed, smiling. "He was all about celebrating Christmas and spending time with the ones you love."

Suddenly, Braden felt inspired. There was something he could do to help the Millers. He could make sure they enjoyed a wonderful holiday season filled with cheer and goodwill. In addition to helping Piper increase business at the Snowy Owl, he would ensure that this Christmas was a memorable one for all of them. A part of him was being self-serving since he knew seeing them reveling in the joy of the season might ease his own suffering. But, in truth, he cared deeply about all of them, especially Piper.

"And that's exactly what we're going to do," Braden chimed in. "We're going to bake holiday pies and hang up holly and mistletoe. And we're all going to wear ugly Christmas sweaters to the holiday stroll and drink peppermint hot cocoa till our stomachs burst. And I just might break out into song. You know I love 'O Come All Ye Faithful.'"

"That's the Christmas spirit!" Trudy exclaimed.

Piper's eyes lit up. "You know how much I love

peppermint hot cocoa with those little marshmallows."

He did indeed. It was one of the things he loved most about her. She got really excited over the small things like hot cocoa and catching snowflakes on her tongue. "We'll stock up on tiny marshmallows," he said, smiling.

From the time they were small kids, Piper had loved all things related to Christmas, especially the food and drinks her father served up at the Snowy Owl. Braden had never seen anyone get more of a kick out of decorating sugar cookies, building gingerbread houses and wrapping presents. This year he wanted her to experience all those cherished holiday memories all over again, to get some relief from all the stress and strain of running a struggling establishment.

It was nice to focus on happy things, Braden realized. For so long now it had been doom and gloom. It didn't assuage his guilt completely regarding Jack's death, but it made him feel a small glimmer of hope. The Snowy Owl could come back from this slump better than ever. After all, Christmas was a time of love and light. And hope! His faith told him he needed to believe in things he couldn't see and that others might not think were even possible.

"I'd hold off on the singing though," Piper teased. "Christmas carols aren't your strong suit."

"Ouch!" Braden said, lifting his hand over his heart. "I'll have you know I've been singing since I was a little tyke."

Piper rolled her eyes. "I know. We stood right next to each other in the church choir. A majority of the time you were warbling off-key."

Braden couldn't help but sputter with laughter. They both knew he had a strong singing voice while Piper's was a bit more problematic. It had been a running theme in their childhood. The choir director had always singled Braden out for praise and solos while Piper had been relegated to the back row. One year during their Christmas concert, Braden had invited Piper to sing his solo with him, leading to a hilarious rendition of "Joy to the World." The choir director had not been pleased by their surprise.

Trudy shook her head at the two of them. "You guys are so silly. It's a good thing you speak the same language."

It was true. He and Piper had always marched in lockstep with each other. He knew her as well as he knew his own face in the mirror. It had always given him comfort, even during the times when he'd felt a bit lost.

"I'd better call it a night," he said after taking a quick look at the time. "I'll be back in the morning to help out. Maybe we can brainstorm about the changes we want to implement around here. Let's make a list of anyone who might be able to help with the pies."

"Night, Braden," Trudy said, hiding a yawn behind her hand. "I better get home myself."

"Thanks for helping out," Piper said, her eyes conveying gratitude.

"That's what friends are for," he responded, nodding before he turned to leave.

Braden heard Piper calling after him. He turned around to see her striding toward him. "Hey! What were you going to tell me earlier before Mama arrived? It seemed pretty intense judging by your expression."

Braden froze. Piper's question totally put him on the spot. With Trudy standing mere feet away, there was no way he felt comfortable baring his soul to her. It was frustrating that he'd finally summoned the courage to come clean, only to have the moment snatched away from him.

"I—I just wanted to tell you I was sorry I bailed so soon after Jack's death. It was selfish of me to leave town. I should have stuck around to support you." Although his words were truthful, they hadn't been the ones he'd wanted to share with her earlier.

Piper frowned. "I appreciate that, but you were a great support system for me when I lost my father. You spent every single day with me in the first few weeks. I was a bit adrift when you left town," she said with a shrug, quickly adding, "but I don't blame you for wanting to live your life as you see fit. I'd be lying though if I pretended your adventures didn't worry me, especially after what happened to my dad."

At that time he hadn't really thought about people worrying about his well-being. He'd only wanted to get as far away from Owl Creek as he possibly could. "I understand. My family felt the same way. I suppose it didn't fully register until I came home and my mother broke down in tears of relief," he admitted. She'd thrown her arms around him and sobbed, confessing that she'd been scared he would never make it back to Owl Creek in one piece.

Piper shook her head, curls bouncing around her shoulders. "Braden, why do I get the feeling there was something more you wanted to say earlier?"

He should have known Piper wasn't going to let his comment go. Piper had a tenacious personality, and it was rare she gave up on anything once it was imprinted on her mind. He didn't know a graceful way out of the situation. He cared about her, but he wished she would just back off!

"Don't you have enough on your plate at the moment without looking for more problems? Let's just concentrate on getting the Snowy Owl financially solvent. That should be your focus instead of trying to read into everything I say and do."

"I'm sorry," Piper blurted out as he wrenched open the door and walked out into the frosty Alaskan evening. He didn't turn back to face Piper, although he truly wanted to give her a hug and tell her she had nothing to apologize for. He was the wrong one. Being around her felt so right at times, while at others it caused feelings of unworthiness to fester inside him. At the moment he felt like the worst person in the world.

Forgive me Lord, he prayed. He hadn't been truthful to Piper just now, and it seemed to him as if he was digging himself a bigger hole each and every day. Braden was angry at himself for allowing his best friend to question her own instincts, but he was so used to covering up now it almost felt like second nature. That was the problem with keeping a secret, he realized. Once you started down the wrong path, it was near impossible to get back on the right one no matter how badly you wanted to.

Chapter Six

By the next morning, Piper had compiled a list of
five people in town who she considered to be seriously gifted bakers. She didn't have much time
to waste in tracking them down since the holidays
were right around the corner. The pie-making oper-
ation needed to get underway immediately in order
to maximize profits.

Unfortunately, after making a few phone calls, only
two people were interested in helping her due to on-
going health issues and other commitments. One of
the ladies who said yes—Birdie McCuller—had
given her a great lead about a treasure trove of pie
recipes owned by an Owl Creek resident. According
to Birdie, Otis's late wife June had been a master-
ful pie baker. Piper had a vague memory of tast-
ing one of her pies at a church picnic. From what
she remembered, June's sweet potato pie had been
a town favorite.

When Braden arrived at the diner, Piper told him

everything she'd discovered about June's stash of pie recipes and the fact that she'd managed to recruit two people to work on baking pies for the diner. Both women had been eager to make a little cash while doing something they loved.

"I'm going to head over to see Otis in a little while. I can't reach him by phone, and I'm eager to ask him if he wouldn't mind sharing those recipes. According to Birdie, they go back several generations. It would be cool to make some really unique pies."

"Can't you just look up some recipes online?" Braden asked, scratching his jaw.

Piper swatted him playfully with her hand. "These recipes are special. You can't beat precious family recipes. They were probably June's pride and joy. I imagine they're sitting in a special tin box in a treasured place at their home. I'd love to tap into them for inspiration."

Braden narrowed his gaze as he looked at her. "So what makes you think Otis will let you use them?"

Piper shrugged. "I don't know for certain, but I think if we both head over there maybe he'll be more willing to share them. Otis is a sweetheart. He won't be able to say no once he sees us face-to-face."

Braden's eyes bulged. "Us? You want me to go with you?" Braden asked. "Who's going to hold down the fort here?"

"Well, it just so happens that Jorge is looking for more responsibility. He's worked here for a long time, but he mainly worked in the kitchen until recently,"

Piper explained, jutting her chin in his direction. At the moment Jorge was working the cash register. In the last few weeks, he'd really come into his own, performing a wide range of duties and showcasing his skills. "He can manage for an hour or so. Things aren't exactly hopping around here," she said, unable to prevent a hint of sadness from creeping into her voice.

Even though she still harbored hope of turning things around at the diner, with each passing day the situation became more precarious. Time was of the essence. If Braden's suggestions didn't work out, she would have to make some heartbreaking decisions. Her mother had been so proud last night watching Piper in her element at the Snowy Owl. She couldn't bear the thought of disappointing her or Hank.

She locked gazes with Braden. Understanding radiated from his eyes. Even though she knew things weren't like they used to be between them, for a moment they seemed to be in perfect sync. Braden knew she was racked with worry. "Okay, let's go pay Otis a visit. I'm driving."

Piper stood up a little straighter. Having Braden by her side made everything better. "Thanks, Braden. You'll see. This trip to see Otis will be worthwhile."

After briefly talking to Jorge, Piper put her winter parka on along with a woolen hat and a pair of cozy Lovely boots. She was now ready for the elements. Outside, Braden yanked open the passenger side door of his car for her. Once he settled himself in the driver's seat, Braden started the car and let it idle for a while to warm up the engine. A cold front had swept in overnight, putting Owl Creek at historically low temperatures for December. Even though she was bundled up, the interior of Braden's vehicle felt frigid.

Otis's house was located about ten minutes from town near the mountains. As they drove past scenic views, Piper's thoughts were racing. Last night she'd stayed up way too late brainstorming ideas for the diner. She'd come up with a plan to have a "countdown to Christmas" promotion where signature holiday items would be served along with a festive giveaway every day. Perhaps a precious ornament, fragrant candle or a festive stocking. And she would tie it in to a theme such as ugly sweaters, Christmas songs or holiday classic films. She wanted to tell Braden all about it, but she needed to focus on the matter at hand—this visit to see Otis.

So much was riding on these next few weeks, and if this pie idea took off, it could be a game changer. Perhaps on the way home she and Braden could brainstorm some more. When they were focusing on the Snowy Owl, Piper could almost pretend as if things were normal between them. It was her fervent hope that working together would bring them back to that place in time when they were completely in sync. And if she managed to hold on to ownership of the diner in the process, it would be the most wonderful Christmas gift of all.

By the time they reached Otis's log cabin, snow was beginning to swirl down from the sky. Piper didn't mind the snow one bit. It wouldn't feel like the holidays without a bunch of the fluffy white stuff gracing Owl Creek. Ever since she was little she'd enjoyed snowstorms and inclement weather. It was one of the many reasons she never wanted to leave Alaska. She felt fortunate to live in the last frontier.

Otis's home was a rustic and charming house, nestled behind a wooded lane. As they drove up to it, the first thing Piper noticed was the smoke curling from the chimney, emitting a cozy vibe. Although it was a sweet cabin, it was clear the place had seen better days. The shutters were a faded gray, and the paint on the front door was chipped and peeling. Piper hadn't been out here in years, not since she'd interviewed Otis for her school paper about his former career as a park ranger. Back then she'd been greeted at the front door by both Otis and June, who couldn't have been a lovelier couple. They had graciously welcomed her into their home and treated her like a treasured guest.

Although neither she nor Braden had spoken about it during the ride over, the trail where her father had suffered his fatal injuries was only a few miles down the road. She'd been acutely aware of it when they were in the vicinity. Actual goosebumps had risen on the back of her neck.

"It must get lonely for Otis living all the way out here by himself," Braden noted, looking around the area as they got out of the truck. All one could see was acres of forest, snowcapped mountains and chopped logs resting in a pile by the house. From the looks of it, Otis would be keeping himself warm for a very long time.

"I imagine so, especially since he's a recent widower. It's so quiet out here," Piper said. "I'm glad my mom had the inn filled with customers to keep her company." She made a mental note to include Otis in more town activities. It couldn't be easy fending for himself after being married for such a long time. She was pretty sure his children, who had children themselves, didn't live nearby.

When they reached the front door, Piper took the lead and knocked. The sound of a barking dog reached their ears. The door swung open to reveal Otis standing on the threshold with a Siberian Husky puppy yipping at his heels. Although Piper wanted to squeal at the sight of the exact type of dog she'd always dreamed of owning, she knew it was important to focus on the matter at hand. Otis raised his hand in a command for the dog. "Settle down, Winter."

His eyes went wide with surprise when he laid eyes on them. "Piper. And Braden. What in the world brings the two of you out to my neck of the woods?"

"We're sorry for the interruption," Piper said, "but may we come in? We have a proposition for you."

Otis took a step back and waved them inside the house. "Of course. Come on in. I'll get the kettle heated so we can have some tea. It's getting pretty nippy out there." Piper and Braden entered the house and took off their snowy boots, leaving them on the mat by the door. "Follow me," Otis said, leading them toward the kitchen. Winter trailed behind them.

The kitchen was warm and bright—yellow walls lent the room a cheery vibe. It had a woman's touch—sweet tea towels and floral tins graced the counter. A wooden sign instructed them to Bless the Cook. Once they'd settled down at the table and Otis had served them their tea along with some zucchini bread, their host cut to the chase.

"So, I'm mighty curious about this proposition you have for me. This is probably the biggest excitement I've had in a long time." Otis's smile was endearing.

Piper shared a quick glance with Braden before speaking. "Otis, I'd like to ask you something, if it's all right."

"You're the biggest sweetheart in town, Piper. You can ask me anything," Otis responded, adding a sugar cube to his tea before stirring it.

Piper warmed at the compliment. "I wanted to know if you still had June's pie recipes. I'm going to start making specialty pies as one of the holiday attractions at the diner." She crossed her hands in front of her and locked gazes with Otis. "I remember how fantastic June's pies were. I seem to recall a very unusual twist on key lime pie, as well. Everyone here in town would always rave about them."

A sheepish expression appeared on his face. He began to fiddle with his fingers while avoiding eye contact with her. "Well, Piper," he said in a halting voice. "I have a confession to make. The truth is it wasn't June who made those pies. It was me." Piper felt her jaw drop. She swung her gaze toward Braden who also seemed flabbergasted by the news.

"You? Why, Otis, that's fantastic," she sputtered.

"Why the secrecy?" Braden asked. "Didn't you want everyone to know about your baking talents?"

Otis looked sheepish. "I grew up in a time when it wasn't considered manly to be a pie baker. I know it sounds ridiculous, but I'm talking fifty years ago in a different time and place. Gender roles were very rigid. So I let June take the credit, even though it drove her crazy not to brag about her pie-making husband. In her eyes I was pretty spectacular."

"Whoa. I did not see that coming," Braden said, letting out a low whistle.

Piper subtly elbowed Braden in the side. "Well, June was right. I think you're amazing, Otis. A true Renaissance man. Would you consider working for me? I've decided to increase my pie supply and frankly, I need help." Piper made a face. "The holiday pies are really important to increasing revenue at the Snowy Owl."

Otis appeared stunned by the invitation. "Do you really want an old guy like me making pies for you?" Otis asked. "These fingers aren't as nimble as they used to be. I have arthritis and a few other ailments."

"It would be an honor, Otis," Piper gushed. "Frankly, I'm eager to up my pie game. I could learn a lot from you."

Otis threw his head back and laughed. "You sure know how to flatter an old man."

Piper wagged her finger at Otis. "My granny always used to say that age is nothing but a number. You've got lots of life in you yet."

"That's right," Braden concurred. "So please say yes to Piper's offer. It would mean the world to her."

"I'd like to show you something." Otis stood up and went over to a cabinet in the corner of the kitchen. After rummaging around in a drawer for a few minutes, he let out a sound of triumph. When he turned back toward them, he was clutching a big scrapbook with frayed edges. He sat back down at the table and lovingly ran his hand over the material. "It's taken me over fifty years of pie baking to compile this book." He let out a ragged sigh. "June gave it to me. She told me I needed to put my recipes in one place so we could pass them down to our children and grandchildren. But Ned and Bonnie don't get back home much, and I barely know my grandkids."

Piper's heart cracked wide open. The loneliness emanating from deep inside Otis threatened to break her. How could she not have known all of this? She saw him several times a week at the diner. It made her feel ashamed of herself for failing Otis. She wanted the diner to be a place where people connected, not only with her but with each other. A tight-knit community of sorts. All the while Otis had been suffering in silence. She'd been so busy worrying about the diner's future, she hadn't noticed the older man's isolation.

She swallowed past a huge lump in her throat. "Sharing the recipes with us is kind of like passing them down, Otis. We've known you our whole lives. When it comes right down to it, you're like an extended member of our family." She wasn't trying to flatter the older man. Everything she'd just said was true.

Otis bowed his head. "Hearing you say that means a lot to me." Tears misted Otis's eyes. He ran a shaky hand over his face. "I'd be happy to work with the two of you. And you're free to use any of my recipes. Things do tend to get a little isolated around here. Working with a team sounds like fun."

"That's wonderful," Piper said, leaning over and pressing a kiss on Otis's cheek. "I'm so thankful you'll be joining us."

She looked up to find Braden's eyes glued on her and Otis. The corners of his mouth were showcasing the beginnings of a smile. She grinned back at him. Things were looking up for her beloved establishment. She had no tangible proof that business would increase, but Braden's assistance at the diner had changed everything. She'd known that recruiting Braden to work with her would yield wonderful ideas.

Their friendship seemed so uncomplicated at the moment. They were working together as a unit toward a common goal, and both of them were putting their best feet forward to salvage her diner. It almost made her believe she'd imagined the distance and tension between them. Deep down she knew she hadn't.

She prayed this moment of tranquility would last, although she feared something would happen to turn everything upside down.

* * *

For much longer than they'd initially planned, Piper and Braden sat with Otis and went through his scrapbook of pie recipes. Braden couldn't bear to tear Piper away when she was clearly enjoying herself. Spending time with Otis was serving as a pick-me-up for her. It was understandable, considering she spent most of her waking hours at the diner. Visiting Otis had provided a well needed break from her day-to-day routine. But they both knew there was a lot of work to do at the diner.

After saying their goodbyes to Otis and arranging for him to come to the Snowy Owl at the end of the week, they began their drive back to town. A few minutes down the road, Piper made a request. "Braden, can you pull over?"

Braden's hands tightened on the wheel as he safely maneuvered the truck to the side of the road. A heavy weight sat on his chest. He didn't need two guesses to figure out why Piper wanted him to stop. *Just breathe*, he reminded himself. *Please, Lord. Give me the strength to get through this without falling apart.*

Piper jumped out of the car and walked toward the base of the trails. She stared off into the distance. "I haven't been back since that day," Piper said, her gaze focused on the mountain.

"Me neither." Braden felt as if he couldn't breathe properly. He hadn't ventured out here since the accident on purpose. His last memory of being up here involved the moments where he'd feverishly tried to save Jack's life. Being this close to the tragic scene felt shattering. Jarring memories flashed before him. He shuddered at the impact. For so long he'd been trying to stuff them down, yet this was proof they hadn't gone anywhere. They'd just roared back to life.

"Piper, why did you want me to stop here? There's nothing here for you but sad memories." He shoved his hands in his pockets and ducked his head. He didn't know how to handle all the feelings coursing through him. Was this God's way of telling him he couldn't run from the past? That he needed to face it head-on before he moved forward? He had avoided this location like the plague, but here he was, standing in close proximity to the accident site.

"I don't know," she answered with a shrug. "This was the place my father felt joy. He loved being up here. He was so busy at the diner, so he rarely had time to go snowmobiling. But every now and again, he would carve out a little bit of time to engage in the things he loved. Sometimes it was heading over to the Avon theater on Main Street with Mama to watch a classic film. Other times he went mushing with his friends from Homer. He was a man who enjoyed life."

"He deserved moments like that. I've never seen a more hardworking man than Jack."

She turned toward him, her eyes full of questions. "You were with him that day. Was he smiling a lot? Happy? Excited about taking a run on his snowmobile?"

Braden winced. How could he possibly answer these questions? If he were to tell her what really happened between him and her father, he knew their friendship would be over. He couldn't imagine a world where Piper wasn't his best friend. But he knew she deserved the truth.

Piper reached out and grabbed his hand. "I'm sorry. I know you were with him after the crash trying to save his life. I can't imagine how terrible those memories must be." She shrugged. "I suppose I'm just looking for something to hold on to, a tiny kernel to help me process losing him in that way. Knowing his last moments were full of happiness helps."

Braden looked down at Piper's hand entwined with his own. He squeezed it, hoping to provide a measure of comfort and reassurance. Piper wanted something he couldn't really give her if he stuck to the truth. But there were shades of gray in the story. Jack had been happy that day. He'd seen him smiling and joking with some townsfolk before he confronted Braden. He knew with a deep certainty that Jack had been in the pursuit of an activity he loved when he crashed.

"Jack was happy that day," he confirmed. "When I first saw him on the mountain, he was surrounded by his buddies. They were teasing him about the few pounds he'd recently gained." Braden chuckled at the memory. "He really took it in great stride and made a comment about having a little more stuffing to play Santa at the holiday stroll."

"That sounds just like him," Piper murmured. "He always looked at the bright side of things. No one embraced the holidays more than he did. It's pretty heartwarming, considering his rough childhood and being in all those foster homes. He never had a real Christmas until he met my mom. She was raising Hank as a single mother after her first husband died. Dad said his whole life changed when he met them." A hint of a smile played at the corners of her mouth. Braden felt relieved she could talk about her father without breaking down in tears, especially considering their location.

He'd always admired Jack and Trudy's relationship. Although he knew no marriage was perfect, they'd made it look effortless. "True love from the sounds of it. I imagine he spent the rest of his life making up for all those holidays he lost out on."

Piper nodded. "He really did. And he had a ball doing it. You have no idea how much you've helped me, Braden. I just wish I'd asked you a long time ago."

"I guess I didn't make it easy for you by leaving town," he said. By taking off from Owl Creek, Braden had been under the belief that he was sparing Piper the cold hard truth of his argument with Jack. In retrospect, perhaps he'd been protecting his own self. And even though he was happy to have given Piper a little bit of closure, guilt still stabbed at him. What he'd just told her wasn't the entire truth. It was a lie of omission.

Braden wasn't sure God would agree with him. He would probably consider it a flat-out falsehood. Matter of fact, he imagined God wasn't very pleased with him for a number of reasons.

After the accident his faith had wavered. He hadn't been able to wrap his head around such a tremendous loss. Jack's passing had created a deep void in his hometown. Piper's grief had nearly swallowed her up whole, and watching her crumble had been gut-wrenching. His own guilt and frustration had spiraled into anger toward God. Why had He allowed Jack to die? Why had God placed Braden up on that mountain to be the focus of Jack's wrath? To this day he still struggled with those questions, along with a host of others.

As he drove back to town, Piper chatted nonstop regarding promotional opportunities for the business. He really liked her countdown to Christmas idea. It was a nice tie-in to the way Jack had run the diner—a nostalgic throwback. But Piper needed to put her stamp on the place in order to move forward. It was fine to honor Jack, but in order to thrive she should carve out her own identity as owner of the Snowy Owl.

"I think it's important to honor the diner's past, but at the same time you've got to make it your own," Braden said. "People need to think of it as your establishment."

Piper winced. "I still think of the diner as belonging to my dad. I can't seem to shake it. My father was such a beloved figure in town. It's like I'm an imposter or something."

Braden stopped the truck at the moose crossing sign. He turned toward Piper, and their eyes held and locked. It wasn't hard to see the raw vulnerability lurking in their depths. He wanted to hold her in his arms and reassure her by telling her she was enough. She didn't have to compete with Jack's legacy. Piper was making her own way and leaving her own special stamp on the diner. "You're nothing of the sort. You're the most genuine and loving person I've ever known. You are the spitting image of Jack. Your heart is just as big as his was. People here in town adore you. Surely you know that."

Piper reached out and touched his hand as it rested on the steering wheel. Braden felt a jolt when her skin brushed against his. For a moment it felt as if an electric current had passed between them. His skin felt all tingly. Feeling stunned, he turned his gaze back toward the road and proceeded to drive back into town. The landscape passed by in a blur. He drove the rest of the way on autopilot.

No matter how hard he tried, Braden couldn't seem to wrap his head around what had just happened. Surely he was imagining things. The little spark of electricity he'd felt between them had come out of nowhere. It had felt like attraction, which completely stunned him. He and Piper had always been in the friend zone. Best friends, in fact. Things between them were already complicated due to the secret he was keeping from her. Adding another layer to their relationship might just push him past the breaking point.

Chapter Seven

The aroma of a dozen holiday pies permeated the air in the diner's kitchen. Piper closed her eyes and sniffed the one she had just taken out of the oven. It was triple berry—blueberries, strawberries and raspberries. Her mouth began to water as she imagined how good it would taste sliding down her throat. "It might be wrong to compliment myself, but this pie smells incredible."

"If you do say so yourself," Braden added with a grin. Piper laughed at the sight of his face smudged with flour. He'd insisted on helping despite his inability to bake. So far she'd witnessed a lot of sampling from where he sat at the table. She had to admit, he was incredibly easy on the eyes. More and more, she was beginning to appreciate that fact. He wasn't a boy anymore. He'd done a lot of growing up in the last few years.

It was after-hours at the diner and Piper had assembled her bakers—Otis, Birdie and Sue McCall—

in order to do a dry run for the holiday rollout. Piper planned to feature the pies at the diner the following day. Pure adrenaline was racing through her veins at the idea of putting it all out there for her customers. She had so much on the line it was almost too frightening to contemplate the situation. There would be at least a dozen fresh varieties ready to go by morning. She couldn't ever remember feeling such a mix of excitement and trepidation.

Piper placed her pie down to cool off on the counter. She walked over to Otis who had lined up all of his in a row. She pointed to the one he'd just taken out of the oven. "That smells out of this world delicious. I can't wait to taste a sliver."

"A sliver?" Otis asked with a chuckle. "This is my favorite. It's eggnog cream. One bite and you're going to be in a state of bliss. Might as well have a whole slice. There's plenty more where that came from." Otis let out a hearty chuckle that reverberated through the kitchen.

"Who am I to argue with that logic?" Piper asked. She would be counting down the minutes while the baked good cooled down. Ever since she was a little girl, she'd had a sweet tooth. The aroma floating around the room left her hankering for a taste.

"I think you've just stumbled upon a great name for it. Bliss pie," Birdie said, smiling flirtatiously at Otis. With her silver hair and tawny skin, Birdie was a good-looking woman. It hadn't escaped Piper's notice that Birdie seemed to be overly fond of the sweet widower. However, Otis appeared oblivious to Birdie's sentiments.

"I think we're all set for the holiday stroll tomorrow," Piper announced. "A dozen pies plus the pizzas will give us a great foundation. Hopefully people will love the pies so much they'll be begging for more." She felt a fluttering sensation in her stomach.

So much was riding on tomorrow. It made her incredibly nervous, yet full of hope that she could turn things around at the Snowy Owl. They were also going to launch the unique milkshakes, which would be Braden's area of expertise. Working on the theory that good things come in threes, Piper also planned to introduce the countdown to Christmas event. She prayed all of her endeavors would be successful.

"Don't forget we're inviting the townsfolk to trim the tree with us," Braden said, pointing toward the boxes of ornaments he'd pulled out of storage earlier that day. "Trudy put together some cranberry and popcorn garlands for us, as well. It's going to be a really festive night."

Piper rubbed her hands together. With every minute that passed, her excitement built up more and more. "I'm not sure I'll get a wink of sleep tonight," she admitted. "There's still so much more to do."

"It's going to be a long day, which is why you need your sleep," Birdie cautioned. "Tomorrow's celebration will be wonderful. I have a feeling this place will be filled to the rafters."

"From your lips to God's ears," Piper murmured. If they hit the ground running with the holiday pies and the milkshakes, it could really result in an increase in the diner's foot traffic. And once customers focused on the diner's new offerings, it might mean they would become regulars.

She bit her lip. Was she hoping for too much? It would be painful if all of her hopes were dashed.

At her request, Braden had hung up Christmas lights outside and placed sprigs of mistletoe by the diner's entrance. It was a nostalgic gesture on her part. How many nights had she witnessed her parents sharing a kiss under the mistletoe? They'd taught her everything she would ever need to know about love everlasting. She prayed often about finding a love story like the one they'd shared. Now that most of her friends were pairing off and settling down, it made Piper realize more than ever that she didn't want to walk through life alone.

"You two are standing under the mistletoe," Sue crowed. "That means you have to kiss."

Birdie let out a little squeal of excitement. "Oh, yes. That's the tradition. Your father used to insist on it, Piper."

"I—I don't think so," she stammered. She felt uncomfortable at the suggestion. Normally she would have just laughed it off. Braden was her close friend after all. What was wrong with her? Why did she feel so put on the spot and jittery? It made absolutely no sense.

"A little peck won't hurt either one of you," Otis added. "Unless there's some reason why you don't want to."

Piper darted a nervous glance at Braden. His face appeared flushed, and he was shifting from one foot to another. His beautiful green eyes were wide with a look resembling alarm. He let out a sigh and took two steps toward her, quickly closing the gap between them. Without any warning, Braden dipped his head down and placed a swift kiss on Piper's cheek. A woodsy scent filled her nostrils as he leaned in. Although it was a fleeting gesture, it rattled Piper. For a few agonizing seconds, it had seemed as if he was going to smack one right on her lips. The moment he pulled away from her, she heard clapping and sounds of merriment.

Braden quickly backed away and stuffed his hands in his pockets. He didn't seem very eager to make eye contact with her. His gaze was focused on the black-and-white parquet floor. "You ready to head out, Otis?" he asked.

"Sure thing, Braden. I'm mighty grateful for the ride home. My night vision on these dark back roads is terrible."

"It's my pleasure," Braden said, placing an arm around the older man. "It's the least I could do since you made me the official pie taster tonight."

"I think that position was self-appointed," Otis responded, garnering laughter from the group.

Piper forced herself to smile and chuckle along with everyone else. Ever since Braden's lips had landed on her cheek, she'd been battling feelings of discomfort. She couldn't even put her finger on why it had been so unsettling, but her stomach was now tied up in knots. She needed to get a grip. Why was she being so fanciful? It was nothing but a peck on the cheek.

But it hadn't felt like nothing. Her cheek felt scorched by Braden's lips. She raised a hand to caress the spot where his lips had been. It still tingled. Everyone streamed out of the diner, and Piper stood in the doorway and waved goodbye as they headed into the night. Once she was alone, she allowed herself the luxury of sinking down onto a chair and putting her feet up. Letting out a sigh, she sat back and rested her head on the table. She was tired. Mentally exhausted in fact. She reckoned her strange feelings about the mistletoe were merely a result of being pushed past her limits. There was nothing more than friendship between her and Braden. And that's exactly how it should be. Her life was already complicated enough. Her relationship with Braden was so full of tension and uncertainty.

Piper didn't have any interest in muddying the waters any further between them. It would be a surefire way to mess up their friendship for good.

On the ride to Otis's house, Braden turned the radio up and played holiday music. He desperately needed to stop thinking about the kiss he'd just placed on his best friend's cheek. Otis tapped his feet and fingers along to the rhythmic beats. The older man reminded him a little bit of his own grandfather. Although Otis was a bit more of an extrovert, the two men shared similar qualities. It was probably the reason why he liked Otis so much.

"There's nothing like Christmas music, is there? I remember the first time I laid eyes on my June it was at a holiday party in Fairbanks. I was stationed at Ladd Air Force Base, and there was a dance there. I looked across the room and there she was, decked out in a red-and-green dress. Once I clapped eyes on her, I saw my entire future flash before my eyes." Otis sounded wonderstruck.

"I can't imagine," Braden said. "I don't really believe in love at first sight, but who am I to disagree? Sounds like the two of you were a true match."

"She was my North Star, Braden. I hope someday you find a woman who'll always lead you in the right direction the way she did. I can't tell you how much I miss her."

"I'm not looking to settle down anytime soon, Otis, but I appreciate the sentiment."

"That Piper is something else, isn't she?" Otis let out a throaty laugh. "She reminds me a little bit of my June. They both have pluck and grit. And incredibly big hearts."

Braden nodded. "I won't argue with you on that. She's been like that ever since she was a kid. She has a heart as big as the great outdoors. You'll never meet a more loyal person." His voice softened. "Or a better friend."

Braden turned off the main road and began driving down the lane leading to Otis's log cabin. Once he stopped the car and put it in Park, he turned to-ward the older man.

"She sounds like a keeper," Otis said, his eyes twinkling.

"She is," he responded before seeing Otis's know-ing smile. "No." He quickly cut Otis off at the pass. "It's not like that. We've been best friends since the cradle."

Otis held up his hands. "Like what? I get the pic-ture. You're just friends. Piper already told me so."

Just friends. It sounded so inconsequential. What he and Piper shared was epic. From the first days of preschool to the triumphant moments of high school graduation, they had been practically inseparable. And unlike some of his other friends, their relation-ship hadn't faltered after graduation. She had con-soled him over his first painful breakup while he had encouraged her to be more confident about her abilities. She was truly one of the only people in the world he completely trusted to be himself with. For so long he'd been feeling unworthy as a member of the North family. Growing up in the aftermath of his sister's abduction had left scars and a heavy dose of survivor's guilt. He'd always been plagued by the question of why Lily had been taken and not him or Connor. Why had he been so blessed? Piper had been the one he'd always leaned on during the tough moments where he had questioned why his family had been forced to go through such an ordeal. Piper had been his rock. Their friendship had been perfect until he'd ruined it.

"Night, Braden," Otis said, reaching for the door handle. "Thanks for going out of your way to bring me home. You're a fine young man. Make sure to tell your parents I said so." With a tip of his hat, Otis exited the truck.

Braden waited until Otis was inside his cabin before turning back down the lane and heading home. He let out a sigh. Otis had been complimentary, but Braden had a hard time accepting his kind words. How would he feel if he knew the secret Braden was keeping? It was doubtful he would be offering him such praise. He was so tired of feeling like a fraud.

He had the distinct feeling Otis had been toying with him about Piper. The grin on his face had spoken volumes. It wasn't the first time someone had teased him about his relationship with Piper, but for some reason it was becoming more difficult to laugh it off as he'd always done in the past. There had been that tense moment earlier when he'd kissed Piper under the mistletoe. It hadn't been anything more than a peck on her cheek, but he couldn't deny that it had felt oddly uncomfortable. He had a feeling he knew exactly why it had been so awkward. The weight of harboring secrets was heavy on his heart, mind and soul. No matter how hard he tried, Braden still couldn't get back to the easy rhythm between him and Piper. Guilt was a strong force, and it reared its ugly head whenever they were in the same orbit.

He prayed the changes he was helping Piper implement at the Snowy Owl would yield great results. It would be his way of making amends for Jack's

"4 for 4" MINI-SURVEY

We are prepared to **REWARD** you with 4 FREE Books and Free Gifts for completing our MINI SURVEY!

Romance

Suspense

You'll get up to...

4 FREE BOOKS & FREE GIFTS

FREE
Value Over
$20!

ıst for participating in our Mini Survey!

Get Up To 4 Free Books!

Dear Reader,

IT'S A FACT: if you answer 4 quick questions, we'll send you 4 FREE REWARDS from each series you try!

Try **Love Inspired® Romance Larger-Print** books and fall in love with inspirational romances that take you on an uplifting journey of faith, forgiveness and hope.

Try **Love Inspired® Suspense Larger-Print** books where courage and optimism unite in stories of faith and love in the face of danger.

Or **TRY BOTH!**

I'm not kidding you. As a leading publisher of women's fiction, we value your opinions... and your time. That's why we are prepared to reward you handsomely for completing our mini-survey. In fact, we have 4 Free Rewards for you, including 2 free books and 2 free gifts from each series you try!

Thank you for participating in our survey,

Pam Powers

To get your 4 FREE REWARDS:
Complete the survey below and return the
insert today to receive up to 4 FREE BOOKS and
FREE GIFTS guaranteed!

▼ DETACH AND MAIL CARD TODAY!

and ™ are trademarks owned and used by the trademark owner and/or its licensee. Printed in the U.S.A.

"4 for 4" MINI-SURVEY

1 Is reading one of your favorite hobbies?
☐ YES ☐ NO

2 Do you prefer to read instead of watch TV?
☐ YES ☐ NO

3 Do you read newspapers and magazines?
☐ YES ☐ NO

4 Do you enjoy trying new book series with FREE BOOKS?
☐ YES ☐ NO

Please send me my Free Rewards, consisting of **2 Free Books from each series I select** and **Free Mystery Gifts**. I understand that I am under no obligation to buy anything, as explained on the back of this card.

☐ **Love Inspired® Romance Larger-Print** (122/322 IDL GQ5X)
☐ **Love Inspired® Suspense Larger-Print** (107/307 IDL GQ5X)
☐ **Try Both** (122/322 & 107/307 IDL GQ6A)

FIRST NAME	LAST NAME

ADDRESS

APT.#	CITY

STATE/PROV.	ZIP/POSTAL CODE

EMAIL ☐ Please check this box if you would like to receive newsletters and promotional emails from Harlequin Enterprises ULC and its affiliates. You can unsubscribe anytime.

Your Privacy – Your information is being collected by Harlequin Enterprises ULC, operating as Reader Service. For a complete summary of the information we collect, how we use this information and to whom it is disclosed, please visit our privacy notice located at https://corporate.harlequin.com/privacy-notice. From time to time we may also exchange your personal information with reputable third parties. If you wish to opt out of this sharing of your personal information, please visit www.readerservice.com/consumerchoice or call 1-800-873-8635. **Notice to California Residents** – Under California law, you have specific rights to control and access your data. For more information on these rights and how to exercise them, visit https://corporate.harlequin.com/california-privacy.

LI/SLI-520-MS20

HARLEQUIN READER SERVICE—Here's how it works:

Accepting your 2 free books and 2 free gifts (gifts valued at approximately $10.00 retail) places you under no obligation to buy anything. You may keep the books and gifts and return the shipping statement marked "cancel." If you do not cancel, approximately one month later we'll send you 6 more books from each series you have chosen, and bill you at our low, subscribers-only discount price. Love Inspired® Romance Larger-Print books and Love Inspired® Suspense Larger-Print books consist of 6 books each month and cost just $5.99 each in the U.S. or $6.24 each in Canada. That is a savings of at least 17% off the cover price. It's quite a bargain! Shipping and handling is just 50¢ per book in the U.S. and $1.25 per book in Canada*. You may return any shipment at our expense and cancel at any time — or you may continue to receive monthly shipments at our low, subscribers-only discount price plus shipping and handling. *Terms and prices subject to change without notice. Prices do not include sales taxes which will be charged (if applicable) based on your state or country of residence. Canadian residents will be charged applicable taxes. Offer not valid in Quebec. Books received may not be as shown. All orders subject to approval. Credit or debit balances in a customer's account(s) may be offset by any other outstanding balance owed by or to the customer. Please allow 3 to 4 weeks for delivery. Offer available while quantities last.

If offer card is missing write to: Harlequin Reader Service, P.O. Box 1341, Buffalo, NY 14240-8531 or visit www.ReaderService.com

BUSINESS REPLY MAIL
FIRST-CLASS MAIL   PERMIT NO. 717   BUFFALO, NY

POSTAGE WILL BE PAID BY ADDRESSEE

HARLEQUIN READER SERVICE
PO BOX 1341
BUFFALO NY 14240-8571

NO POSTAGE
NECESSARY
IF MAILED
IN THE
UNITED STATES

death and moving past it. Braden wasn't foolish enough to think he could ever repair the damage he'd wrought, but he would be doing a kindness for Piper and helping her turn a page. Losing the diner would be like losing Jack all over again. If that happened, he wasn't certain how Piper would survive it.

Piper woke up the following morning to the savory scent of coffee wafting under her nose. She let out a groan and crawled back under her duvet cover. This was the problem with having flannel sheets, she realized. She felt way too warm and cozy to get up in order to open the diner. A light knock sounded on her bedroom door. "Come in," she said before the knob began to turn, and her mother walked in carrying a tray filled with breakfast goodies.

"Good morning, sweetheart," Trudy called out. "I have a treat for you. You've been working so hard these last few days I've barely seen you."

Piper sat up in bed and propped herself against the bed frame. Trudy walked over and placed the tray on Piper's lap. "This is so sweet, Mama," she said, looking down at the steaming cup of coffee and a plate filled with eggs, waffles and bacon. "But I'm not going to be able to savor it. I have to get going to the Snowy Owl. It's going to be a long day."

Trudy sat down on the bed beside Piper. "You're going to be on your toes all day and evening due to the holiday stroll, but you don't have to go in for a few hours." Trudy's grin stretched across her face. "Jorge is opening up the diner this morning. He wanted to do something nice for you due to all the extra hours you've been putting in. Isn't he a sweet-heart?"

Piper was a bit of a control freak about the diner, but she didn't have the energy to protest. She would love to stay in her pj's for another hour of rest and relaxation. Plus, she trusted Jorge implicitly. He was a wonderful man and a hard worker. The Snowy Owl was in good hands with him at the helm.

"I'm going to let you relax for a bit and eat your breakfast. I've got some laundry to take care of. I'll be on hand tonight if you need my help." She sent Piper a tender smile. "Your dad and I used to have so much fun at this event. It was always such a cele-bration of Christmas and our good fortune. We were blessed beyond measure to find each other. I hope one day you find someone as solid as him to spend your life with."

"Me too," Piper murmured as her mother pressed a kiss against her temple and headed out the door, closing it firmly behind her.

Piper dug in to her meal and sipped the hazelnut-flavored coffee. It was a real treat to indulge in breakfast in bed without having to worry about the diner. Lately she'd allowed it to consume her, and she knew going forward things would have to change. Once the Snowy Owl got on its feet, she intended to implement some changes.

The sound of footsteps echoed on the stairs. There was always a lot of hustle and bustle at the inn in the morning as guests settled in for breakfast in the dining room.

"I have another surprise for you," Trudy crowed, her eyes twinkling with mischief.

Suddenly, Rachel was standing in the doorway. With her beautiful features and lovely smile, her friend was the type of person who made quite an impression. She and her husband, Gabriel, were raising her twin daughters, Faith and Lizzy. Rachel was living proof that second chances did exist. Despite having made mistakes along the way, Rachel had walked off into the sunset with her one true love.

"Rachel. What are you doing here?" Piper felt a groundswell of emotion seeing her close friend. Due to their busy schedules they hadn't been able to spend as much time with each other as either would have liked. Piper had been over the moon when Rachel had decided to stay in Owl Creek with her girls after a three-year absence from town.

"I'm here making a house call. One of the guests isn't feeling well. Her symptoms indicate she's suffering from a stomach bug, but I'm fairly certain she'll be feeling better in twenty-four hours. I was all too happy to swing by and check on her." Rachel gave Piper a quick hug. "I was hoping our paths would cross."

"Being married looks good on you," Piper said, giving Rachel the once-over.

Rachel beamed. "I'm glad it shows. I never imagined coming back home would give me the life I've always dreamed of having."

"No one deserves it more than you and Gabriel," Trudy chimed in. "And those adorable girls of yours." Piper's mother placed her arm around Rachel's waist and pulled her in for a squeeze. "Excuse me, ladies. I have to go make sure there's enough syrup on the table for the waffles."

"She really loves running the inn," Piper said with a grin as she watched her mother head out of the kitchen. She hoped people saw the same enthusiasm in her regarding her management of the Snowy Owl. Despite the ongoing financial strain, she could truly say she loved her job. God willing, the diner would be around for a very long time so she could pass it down to her own children. But first she needed a little romance in her life. It would be impossible to settle down if she wasn't even dating.

"Gabriel and I were wondering if you needed any help with the holiday stroll? We'll have the girls in tow, but we can still pitch in."

Piper clapped her hands. "Oh, that would be wonderful, Rachel. The more the merrier. Braden has been working with me to come up with some ideas to increase business and perk up our menus. He's been really helpful."

Rachel wrinkled her nose. "Are those new restaurants in town still giving you trouble?"

"Let's just say the competition is fierce." Excitement rushed through her. "But Braden suggested I increase my pie production. We're going to roll them out tonight for the holiday stroll, then make some available for the diner." She shook her head and giggled. "And he has this epic idea to create these crazy milkshakes." She put her hands together in prayer-like fashion. "Praying it all works out."

"You seem so happy. I'm glad you and Braden are reconnecting. I know you were a bit confused and hurt when he appeared to be avoiding you."

Piper hadn't forgotten all of those wounded feelings. They rested just beneath the surface. On occasion they still pricked at her heart. Rachel was the only one she'd confided in about how deeply Braden's actions had affected her. "I still sense there's something off between us. Even though we're working together it's as if there's this veil over him. He's just not the old Braden I've spent so much time with over the years."

Rachel frowned. "Do you think he's hiding something?"

Piper bit her lip and nodded. "Yes, I do. Although I have no idea what it could be. I can't quite put my finger on it. What could have happened to make him want to steer clear of me for such a long time? I hope I don't sound paranoid, but he was gone from Owl Creek for so long. It just seemed as if he was running away from something."

"Don't shoot the messenger, but do you think he has romantic feelings for you? Sometimes those lines get blurred."

Piper scrunched up her face. "No, I really don't. We've always been just friends even though—" She stumbled over her words and stopped talking. Piper wasn't sure she should mention the harmless smooch from the other night.

Rachel pounced on her slipup. "Even though what?"

"We were at the diner the other night and a few of my bakers were urging us to kiss under the mistletoe. He gave me a peck on the cheek, and this really strange energy surrounded us. I think we both felt awkward and uncomfortable."

"Well, that's not really odd considering you've been best friends since you were in diapers. Add in Braden's disappearing act from Owl Creek and the fact that you haven't been in sync lately. Honestly, it's no small wonder it all feels a bit strained."

"It's not like that all the time. Sometimes it seems as if everything is back to normal between us, which is lovely." A ragged sigh slipped past her lips. "We'll end up laughing over a funny joke or reminiscing about something from the past. I wish those moments outweighed the ones that make me question what's going on with him."

"I've learned with my profession that we never know what another person is going through. I know the two of you always told each other your deep dark secrets, but sometimes things shift. Don't forget his long-lost sister returned out of the blue not too long ago. Although it's a blessing she's been reunited with the Norths, it probably brings back a lot of traumatic memories. Braden is the strong silent type. There's no telling what feelings he's been suppressing."

Piper felt a sinking sensation in her gut. Her problems with the diner had felt so all-consuming that she hadn't paused to consider what Braden had been going through for the past few months. Piper knew all too well that the abduction of his baby sister had left scars he'd always attempted to hide from his family. Sage's return had been a blessing, but it had brought to light the evil deeds committed by the woman who had stolen Sage, then raised her as her own child. There was no question in her mind he must still be grappling with the situation and trying to make sense of it all.

She vowed to do better at supporting Braden. If he needed a shoulder to lean on, she would provide it. Although she agreed with Rachel about the stress of Sage's return to Owl Creek, Piper still couldn't manage to convince herself that it was related to Braden's aloof behavior. Every instinct told her it had something to do with her. And she still worried that this secret Braden was keeping might forever alter their friendship.

Chapter Eight

Owl Creek's town square was lit up in shimmering lights, twinkling stars and festive garlands. A massive Christmas tree stood in the middle of the town green. It was a tradition to turn on the tree lights at the conclusion of the holiday stroll event. Everywhere he looked, Braden spotted signs of holiday bling. Kids were riding sleighs led by Alaskan malamutes and Siberian huskies. His grandparents were dressed up as Santa and Mrs. Claus. Braden chuckled as he watched kids scrambling to sit on Santa's lap and make their heartfelt wishes.

He didn't think he'd ever seen so many wreaths in his entire life. There were dozens hanging up all around Main Street. It seemed as if the whole town had shown up to support the local businesses and spread holiday cheer throughout the village. He'd been manning a table with Piper they'd set up on the town green. In a while he would head to the diner and get down to the business of making some of his supreme holiday shakes to lure customers inside the Snowy Owl after the holiday stroll.

"I can't believe how many people turned out," Piper said. "We're about to run out of pie samples."

Braden raised his hand in the air. "Yes! Leave them wanting more." He flashed a smile at Piper. It was wonderful seeing all of their hard work come to fruition. "I have the feeling a lot of pie orders will be coming in over the next few days."

"That would be wonderful," Piper said, clapping her mittened hands together.

"The feedback has been terrific. Owl Creek has gone pie crazy," Braden said, making a goofy face at Piper.

She swatted at him, chuckling. "You look like you're five years old."

"Aww, c'mon," Braden said, placing his hand over his heart. "You hurt my feelings." Piper rolled her eyes and let out a snort.

"Brrr. It's so cold out here I feel like my feet are turning into icicles." Piper began jumping up and down. "If I stand still for too long, I literally cannot feel them."

"Why don't we head inside? The pie is pretty much a wrap. There's only that one little slice of apple left. Between the two of us, we could polish it off in no time."

Piper giggled. "How many slivers have you eaten tonight? Wait. Here comes Mrs. Crenshaw. I happen to know she loves apple pie."

He'd always loved the sound of her laughter and

what it did to her face. It transformed her pretty features into radiant ones. Ever since his return to Owl Creek, Braden had been viewing his best friend with a whole new pair of eyes. Growing up she'd been a tomboy, running around with skinned knees and faded, ripped blue jeans. Now he imagined the men in town were tripping all over themselves to date her. His protective instincts kicked into high gear. He would run interference if he had to in order to protect Piper from anyone who didn't have the best of intentions.

"Earth to Braden!" Piper was waving her hand in front of his face. "Where did you go just now? Our last slice of pie is history. Let's go inside the diner before we freeze our tootsies off."

"You don't have to tell me twice," Braden said, grabbing some of the empty disposable plates while Piper cleared away the rest. "Race you to the door," Braden said as he took off running toward the diner.

"No fair," Piper called out after him. "You had a head start."

"No sour grapes allowed," Braden shouted, looking over his shoulder to see Piper gaining on him. In an effort to make sure she didn't pass him, Braden attempted to sprint the last one hundred yards. Ever since they were little they'd been competitive with one another over the silliest of things. This would be no different. Suddenly, he hit a patch of icy snow and his legs slipped out from underneath him. He landed with a thud.

Instead of helping him up, Piper was bent over at

the waist chortling with laughter. "This is what you get for being so full of yourself."

"Seriously? You're going to lecture me instead of helping me up?"

"I'm sorry, Braden. Are you all right?" Piper asked. She lowered her hand and with a grunt helped him to a standing position. Once Braden stood up, he let out a groan and massaged the back of his thigh. "Yeah, I'm fine," he said, dusting snow off his pants. "My ego is just a little bruised. I do extreme adventures all over the world, but I can't run in a little Alaskan snow?"

Piper linked arms with him. "Aww. You're still a rock star, Braden. King of extreme sports and out of this world milkshakes." She put a hand to her forehead in dramatic fashion. "Rescuer of damsels in distress."

Braden chuckled. "You don't need saving, Piper. If you put your mind to it, you could conquer the world."

"Remember when we wanted to be superheroes? I used to love dressing up as Wonder Woman," Piper said, reminding him of all the dreams they'd shared over the years. He hoped those days weren't over. It would make him really happy if he and Piper could be a part of each other's lives till they were old and sitting on their porches in rocking chairs. Just the thought of it made him grin. He could imagine Piper with salt-and-pepper hair and a few little crinkles around her eyes.

"Those were the days," he said. "It felt like anything was possible."

Piper turned around to face him. "It still is, Braden. If it wasn't, I would have just given up trying to turn things around at the diner. Because of you I'm still fighting to save it."

Once again, he was forced to stuff down feelings of guilt. Accepting Piper's praise felt self-indulgent. He still felt unworthy of her compliments. He knew all too well she wouldn't be praising him if she knew the truth. Which made him a fraud.

Piper led the way up the stairs, then pulled open the doors to the Snowy Owl. He heard her shocked exclamation. She stopped in her tracks and didn't enter the establishment.

"What's happening?" Piper turned toward him, eyes wide with shock. He quickly moved to her side so he could see what was wrong. Piper seemed to be in a state of shock.

The diner was packed to the rafters with customers. People were standing around waiting for seats while every booth and table was occupied. Even the counter seats were completely filled up. The staff was busy servicing customers and bustling from table to table.

"I think we've got a sellout crowd," Braden crowed. The look etched on Piper's face was priceless. She appeared shell-shocked. He lightly jabbed her in the side. "Smile, Piper. This is exactly what you wanted to happen."

"I—I never expected this crush of people. It feels

a little overwhelming," she confessed. Braden gently pushed her over the threshold and leaned down to whisper in her ear, "Just breathe."

Jorge, looking a little frazzled, rushed over to them. "I don't think I've ever been so happy to see two people in my life. We're filled to capacity and completely out of pies. People aren't just ordering slices. They're buying whole pies and placing orders." Jorge wiped a hand across his brow. "At this rate we'll be filling requests all through January."

Braden let out a celebratory hoot. "That's amazing news."

Jorge placed a hand on his shoulder. "Braden, everyone is waiting for the milkshakes. There's been a slight frenzy about them," he explained. "People are really eager to put their orders in."

Braden rubbed his hands together. "I'm on it. Give me a few minutes to take my coat off, wash my hands and get situated."

Jorge nodded, then darted off to a nearby table to handle a party of six.

"I'm going to figure out how to make some more seating so people aren't just standing around," Piper said, shooting him a tremulous smile. "Let's do this. God listened to my prayers and sent customers into the Snowy Owl. The very least we can do is feed them."

Piper stood a few feet away from the fully decked out Christmas tree, admiring the way it shimmered and twinkled with red and green lights. A shiny gold star sat on top. The Snowy Owl had seen a steady stream of foot traffic in the past few hours. All the ornaments had been hung on the tree along with every garland Trudy had brought over from the inn. So many people had shown up to help trim the tree and order pies and milkshakes Piper could hardly believe it. Although Braden had been making milkshakes non-stop, he'd finally served up his last treat.

Hank, Sage and Piper's niece, Addie, were sitting at a booth with Gabriel, the twins and Connor. Rachel was manning the counter and taking pie orders with Piper's mother. All of the Norths had shown up. Braden's parents, Willa and Nate, seemed to be radiating sheer happiness. It would be the first Christmas they shared with their newfound daughter. Piper knew it would be extra special for all of them. Although it still ached to not have her dad around during the holidays, Piper felt such joy for the Norths.

She watched as Braden headed over to the jukebox and turned up the music. The strains of "Rocking Around the Christmas Tree" began to ring out in the diner. Braden walked over to his grandmother and held out his hand. Although Beulah tried to wave him off, Braden wasn't taking no for an answer. He took Beulah's hand and pulled her toward an open space near the tree where he began twirling her around to the upbeat rhythms. Moments later Braden's grandfather tapped Piper on the shoulder and invited her to the makeshift dance floor. Although the space was very small, it soon filled up with throngs of dancers.

The vibe in the diner was heartwarming and uplifting. Before too long it was Beulah and her husband dancing cheek to cheek all alone in the middle of the diner. Piper let out a sigh. Braden stood a few feet away with his sister. The expression on his face as he watched his grandparents was touching. He looked exactly like the pint-size version of himself from their younger years—he was staring at them as if they were constellations in a star-filled sky. She felt a pang in her heart as she gazed at him. None of this would have been possible without Braden's support and vision.

As the night wound down, everyone bundled up and headed outside for the tree lighting. Piper locked up the diner behind her. Despite the plummeting temperatures, a large crowd gathered on the town green. The velvety night sky was sprinkled with twinkling stars. Looking around her caused a feeling of warmth and light to flow through Piper. For so many reasons she'd dreaded the holiday season, but tonight had shown her that despite the huge hole her family would never be able to fill, they had so much to be thankful for. Family. Friends. Townsfolk. A feeling of gratitude swelled inside her.

Dear Lord. Thank You for blessings both big and small. I have so much to be grateful for, especially during this holiday season. Today showed me that I'm way more loved than I ever realized. And even though things are far from being fixed at the diner, You gave me a spirit of hope.

As the crowd thinned out and people began to head home, Piper found herself still relishing the camaraderie of the evening. Even though she was tired, she was still having fun talking to old friends and sharing the news about the diner's countdown to Christmas events.

"Hey, shouldn't you be heading home? You must be exhausted." Braden had walked over to where she was standing admiring the Christmas lights. There were only a handful of residents still hanging around, and even though it was nearing midnight, she wanted to savor the bliss of this very special evening.

"I think on some level I didn't want this to end. All is calm and bright and beautiful. It's been an incredible night, hasn't it?" Piper asked. "I couldn't have asked for more."

"You pulled off a spectacular event. Everyone went crazy over your holiday pies. Rachel could barely keep up with the orders."

"And what about your incredible milkshakes? They were as much in demand as the pies. The diner made more money tonight than on any other night over the last four years."

Braden let out a low whistle. "Take a bow. You did it, Piper. If this continues, the diner will be in great shape before you know it."

"I don't want to get carried away, but I'm hopeful. Tonight made me feel like anything is possible."

She felt breathless with excitement. Instead of wringing her hands about the diner, she was actually being proactive about solving her problems. And it was working. It felt amazing to put your faith in something and have it confirmed. Her belief in

Braden had been validated. "I didn't do it on my own. It was your idea to focus on holiday pies. We've always been a great team."

"We have, haven't we? Remember our science project in fourth grade?" Braden's eyes twinkled with merriment.

Piper let out a groan. "Of course, I do. We frittered away our time and with one week to go we decided to kick it into high gear. We ended up making a demo of Mount Kilauea erupting."

Braden clutched his stomach and let out a chuckle. "I'll never forget the look of shock on Miss Beale's face when the lava started overflowing like crazy. It was sheer pandemonium in the classroom."

"We added too much baking soda. Rookie mistake."

"True, but we ended up getting an honorable mention ribbon and our photo was in the *Owl Creek Gazette*. It worked out way better than we ever imagined."

"That's why I asked you to help me in the first place. You always get the job done." Her grin had to be completely taking over her face. Hope was such a precious commodity, and tonight made her so excited about the Snowy Owl's future. Suddenly, things didn't seem so bleak. Braden always made her believe nothing was impossible. Despite their issues, there was no one else in creation who made her feel this way.

Braden shook his head. "Your idea about letting the townsfolk trim the Christmas tree at the diner was pure genius. You made everyone feel as if they were a part of things. And then people started ordering the milkshakes and sticking around for dinner. It was sheer holiday perfection."

Piper rubbed her mittened hands together. "That's what it felt like to me. Everyone came together to celebrate this joyous season. My family and yours, friends, residents, tourists. It couldn't have worked out any better." She let out a little squeal of happiness. Tonight had been wonderful! And empowering. She was filled with anticipation about Christmas and the possibility of what the future might bring. For so long now she'd been stuck in the past, in large part due to her father's untimely passing.

Although grief was a long road to travel with many ups and downs along the journey, this Christmas felt different. The memories weren't choking her. Instead, she was learning to cherish them.

"It was a brilliant evening. You're the perfect person to run the diner, Piper." His eyes radiated warmth and pure joy. "You're carrying on Jack's legacy with so much heart and soul. If he could see you now, he'd be bursting with pride." His voice cracked with emotion. "Don't ever doubt yourself. Because honestly, I never have."

Braden made her feel like she was a rare gem. Praise from his lips felt like the heat of a thousand suns beating down on her. A celebratory feeling hung in the air, and the future was ripe with promise. Hope was such a precious gift. For so long she had put it on the back burner as if it wasn't even a possibility in her circumstances. She was learning that there were certain things one should never give up on. Braden had reminded her of that.

At the moment her heart was so full with gratitude, almost to the point of overflowing. She feared it just might burst. "I've always felt kind of ordinary, but you make me feel like I'm one of a kind. That's a rare talent, Braden North."

"Ordinary?" he scoffed. "Nothing could be further from the truth. You're special, Piper. I've traveled all over the world, and I've yet to meet anyone more spectacular than you."

Despite the frigid temperature, Piper's cheeks warmed at the compliment. Something shifted between them in the moment, and Piper knew instinctively that Braden felt it too. It was as powerful as the northern lights shimmering in the heavens. The scent of pine hung in the air, serving as a fragrant reminder of the season. She tilted her face upward, just as Braden dipped his head down. As his lips moved over hers, she kissed him back with equal measure, relishing the sweet surprise. *This*, she thought. This kiss felt so right, as if she'd been waiting to experience it her entire life. With the snow swirling all around them and the twinkling lights from the Christmas display providing a lovely backdrop, the moment couldn't have been more romantic. It felt to Piper as if the sky had suddenly opened up to reveal countless stars.

Kissing your best friend wasn't smart for a number of reasons, but she couldn't deny how right it felt. She couldn't remember ever experiencing such a wonderful smooch. Perhaps it was their history as best friends or maybe there was just something about Braden that made it special.

By the time the kiss ended and they broke away from one another, Piper felt warm all the way down to her toes. It was a heady feeling. Never in a million years had she expected the night to end with this sensational kiss.

She looked up at Braden, startled by the tense expression stamped on his face.

"I shouldn't have kissed you," he said in a shaky voice. "It was a mistake." Braden's cheeks were flushed, and his eyes held a dazed look. Piper kept quiet as she struggled to absorb Braden's words. A mistake? Her chest tightened. She clenched her hands at her sides. She was mortified. And completely baffled by the sudden turn of events.

"We're friends, Piper. We've always been the best of friends and nothing should ever get in the way of that." There was a sharpness to his tone she rarely heard. *Who was this man?* Where had Braden gone? Suddenly, she was no longer floating on air. Braden's words had caused her to crash back down to earth with a bang.

She felt like an idiot. Her stomach was tied up in knots. She knew things were complicated since they were friends, but it hurt to know Braden regretted kissing her. He seemed to be in such distress over it. Anger spiked through her. What he'd just said didn't make any sense. Hadn't something gotten between them over the last three and a half years? He'd erected a solid wall that she hadn't been able to penetrate.

Hurt rose up inside her, and she couldn't find an adequate response to his declaration. It was so confusing to be kissing him one moment and then feeling angry at him a few seconds later. It was disappointment and rejection all rolled up into one. How could someone she cared about so deeply wound her so much? He'd been the one to initiate the kiss, yet now he was distancing himself from it…and her.

"I haven't told my family yet, but I might not be staying in Owl Creek." His face was shuttered as he made his bombshell announcement.

Shock roared through her. Braden was leaving town again? He had just reunited with his long-lost sister after decades of separation. "You're thinking about leaving town? Why? You've barely been back for any time at all." Once again her radar went up. He wasn't making any sense at all.

Braden shrugged. "I love being at home and I want to seize the opportunity to get to know Sage better, but I don't want to follow the path my family has set out for me. You know me better than anyone. Can you really see me sitting in a corporate office all day?" Braden winced and shook his head. "A part of me feels ashamed to be rejecting the family business, but I can't be something I'm not." There was pain laced in his voice. She hated seeing him so lost.

Truthfully, Piper did have a hard time imagining him being cooped up in an office, although she knew it had always been Beulah's dream to have the entire family working for North Star Chocolates. With Sage's return to Owl Creek, the Norths had been excited to see the dream finally come to fruition. That had to be weighing heavily on Braden's mind. She knew he must feel a sense of obligation to his relatives, particularly in light of what they'd endured.

The Norths were tight-knit, and she knew how tough it would be for Braden to walk away from the family legacy. But it would be even harder for the rest of them to see him leave Owl Creek yet again. They would be incredibly hurt by his decision. "I understand your reservations, but that doesn't mean you have to go away again," she said in an urgent tone. "Stay and figure things out. Here you are assisting me with my problems with the diner, while you're clearly struggling. Let me help you, Braden."

His features hardened, and he took a step away from her. "You can't help me with this, Piper. It's not something anyone can fix. I simply have to do what's right for me. I don't belong in Owl Creek anymore. I need to map out my life somewhere else."

A chill swept through her. His words sounded so final, as if he was fully prepared to leave his hometown permanently. Every instinct in Piper told her that Braden wasn't simply leaving due to his desire to break free from his family's expectations about running the chocolate company. There were other things he could do in his hometown and many different dreams to pursue. It wasn't Braden's way to give up so easily. It was clear that something was eating him up inside.

"What's really going on, Braden? What aren't you telling me?" Piper asked, her voice beseeching him to tell her the truth. She reached out and grasped his sleeve, determined to make him stick around and talk this out. Not knowing was driving her a little bit crazy. Her imagination was beginning to run amok. "We've always been able to tell each other everything. What's changed?"

"We were kids then," he said testily, pulling away from her grip. "You can't expect everything to stay the same, Piper. Life doesn't work that way. I wish it did, but it doesn't." With a shake of his head, Braden turned away and began walking back toward Main Street. His jerky movements were full of frustration and anger. Once again, he'd left her feeling crushed.

As he stormed away, Piper inhaled a deep, steadying breath. His words had cut her to the core. Piper knew she hadn't imagined their tight bond. Everyone in town had borne witness to it. If Braden didn't care about her, he wouldn't be helping her turn things around at the Snowy Owl. Piper knew she wasn't a fanciful person. She'd always been firmly rooted in reality. Something wasn't right.

Always trust your instincts. Those words of advice had been given to her by her father many years ago, and she'd always made it a point to heed his wise counsel.

She couldn't let go of the feeling that Braden was hiding something from her. She'd felt this way for a long time now, and it was only heightening as time went by. Her mind overflowed with questions. Why would he be taking off again when he'd only just returned? Wasn't this his chance to bond with Sage and celebrate the Norths being one big whole family again? He was a hometown boy who'd always adored Owl Creek. What was he running from? What was so wrong that he couldn't stick around and face it head-on?

Piper pressed her hand against her chest. She was battling a sharp pain that wouldn't let up. The very thought of losing Braden made her want to sob and kick and scream. Just when she was beginning to count on him, he was going to disappear from her life. And in leaving Owl Creek he would be breaking her heart all over again.

Chapter Nine

All the way home Braden chided himself for kissing his best friend. What in the world had come over him? It had been a stupid and impulsive act. Without a doubt, any man in his right mind would be over the moon to kiss a woman like Piper, but he wasn't just anyone. The secret he was harboring complicated the situation. It had him so tied up in knots he was actually considering the idea of leaving Owl Creek again so he wouldn't hurt Piper any more than he already had. After all, he'd done it once before.

More and more he was realizing how much Piper had blossomed from his gangly sidekick into a stunningly beautiful woman. For so long he'd gazed at her through the lens of a childhood friend. Now, with each and every day, his eyes were opening more and more about the strong and independent woman Piper had become over the past few years.

There wasn't a single thing about her he didn't

cherish. She had pluck and grit, and she brightened any room she entered.

The random impulse to kiss her had caught him off guard. He'd acted on pure yearning. But it had been all wrong. There were just so many reasons he shouldn't have done it. Crossing lines in their friendship wasn't wise. Piper had always felt like home to him, but he had to tread carefully with her. He didn't want to risk blurring the lines between friendship and romance. And with this huge secret sitting between them, he shouldn't have made a big move like that.

But resting right under the surface was the knowledge of how right it had felt.

He banged his hand against the steering wheel. Now things were going to be incredibly strained between him and Piper. It had been awkward ever since he'd arrived back in Owl Creek, but this would be ten times worse. No woman ever wanted to be told that kissing her had been a mistake. He wouldn't blame Piper if she never wanted to speak to him again.

Every time he felt as if things were sliding into place between them, something happened to cause him to backslide. Perhaps they'd never totally get back on track. It would be devastating, but he knew it was a possibility.

As Braden pulled up to the family compound, he noticed that the interior of the house was dark, with the exception of a multitude of colored lights decorating the pine tree in front of the house. Braden let himself inside, quickly noticing a soft light emanating from the kitchen. Following the trail of light, Braden ended up standing in the doorway looking at his father as he sat down at the kitchen counter with a plate of sugar cookies and a large glass of milk. Tenderness rose up inside him at the sight of his dad. Nate North was a good man, one who'd raised him and Connor with strong values and a deep sense of the importance of family. Time and again Braden asked himself how his father had survived his sister's kidnapping. When he'd once asked him that question as a little kid, Nate hadn't hesitated to answer. "Faith, my boy. Pure faith." He'd never forgotten those words, and he knew that he never would. It had taught him about believing in something with an unshakable dedication.

"What are you doing up? Midnight snack?" Braden asked as he opened the fridge and took out the bottle of milk and then poured himself a generous glass. He turned back toward his father, smiling at the way he was dunking his cookies into his glass.

"I was actually waiting up for you," Nate said, patting the chair next to him. "Take a seat, son. I'd like to talk to you." His father's blue eyes bore into him intently.

"What's going on?" Braden asked as he sat down beside him. He had a funny feeling he was going to be grilled. It wasn't every day his father stayed up late to have an audience with him.

"You tell me. I've been biding my time, but I didn't want to wait another day before asking you how you're doing." Nate's brows were knit together.

His eyes radiated concern. It was the last emotion he wanted his father to feel. For twenty-five years Nate had worried about the fate of baby Lily. It wrecked Braden to think he was the cause of his father's alarm.

"I'm fine, Dad," he said, trying to make his voice sound steady.

Nate shook his head. "No, Braden. I don't think you are. Ever since you left Owl Creek to chase high-flying adventures I've wondered and worried about you. You've been running from something." His father reached out and placed his hand on Braden's. "Talk to me. Tell me what's going on."

Braden bowed his head. He couldn't look his father in the eye and tell him a lie. He was far from being fine. That was for sure. But how could he tell him what had happened that day on the mountain? He didn't want to put any more burdens on his father's shoulders. He'd carried enough to last a lifetime.

"You're right, Dad," he admitted, dragging his gaze up to lock eyes with Nate. "There's something that happened a few years ago and I've kept it a secret. I'm not proud of it. It doesn't sit well within my soul, and I'm trying to make amends for it."

"Care to elaborate?" Nate asked, his dark brows furrowed.

"I don't think I'm ready to share, Dad. I'd like to tell you everything…down the road. Just not right now."

"And Piper? How does she fit into all of this? I

couldn't help but notice there was a distance between you for the last few months."

"Was it that obvious?" he asked. It was a slightly uncomfortable feeling knowing the entire town might be gossiping about his relationship with Piper. And here he'd thought virtually no one had noticed.

"I doubt most people gave it a second thought, but you're my son. I'll always care about what's going on in your world." His father's steely gaze never left him. It was clear he was still seeking an answer to his question.

"It involves her," he admitted. "She's still my best friend, but I'm afraid I'm going to lose her." The very thought of it made his heart constrict. It felt like he was on a runaway train he couldn't stop from careering off the tracks.

"Because of this…secret?" his father pressed.

Braden nodded. "I thought by helping her with the diner I could make amends, but I still feel such guilt. And I don't have the courage to tell her what she needs to know."

"Are you being prayerful about it? God knows what you're going through. If you can't tell me or Connor or even Piper, make sure you tell Him. He will guide you home."

Braden felt moisture welling up in his eyes. *Home.* For so long he had been homesick for this very place. Alaska was firmly rooted in his identity, as was being a member of the North family. Being able to come back to Owl Creek had been his heart's desire for a long time. But it hadn't turned out to be as idyllic as he'd imagined. Time hadn't healed all of Piper's wounds, and the ones he was carrying around still weighed heavily on him.

"I do talk to Him. All the time. I'm struggling a bit to understand why terrible things happen to good people. No matter how much I toss it around in my mind, nothing seems to make sense. It makes me so mad and frustrated."

Nate grasped his hand and squeezed it tightly. "I've been about as low as a man can be after our child was stolen from us. I was angry at God for allowing someone to steal Lily right from our own home where she should have been safe and sound. At times I was so bitter and enraged I could hardly see straight. But a wise man gave me some sound advice I've never forgotten. It's okay to be angry, but don't stay that way. Walk with Him."

Braden closed his eyes and began to fervently pray. *Lord, please show me the way. Give me the courage to be the man I want to be. Let me stick this thing out with Piper and help her get the diner in a solid place before I tell her the truth.*

Why did it seem as if his attempt at redemption was stalled? Helping Piper with the diner wasn't alleviating any of his guilt. Perhaps there was only one way to truly find the closure he was seeking. He knew now what he had to do. Whether he stuck around town or not, he needed to be completely honest with Piper. He would wait until after Christmas and then tell her what he'd been holding on to for the last four years. Then and only then would he be able to look her in the eye and know he was being a friend in the truest sense of the word.

Piper had no idea how she was going to last all day at the diner without looking at Braden. Ever since he'd shown up this morning, she'd been avoiding being alone with him or making more than minimal eye contact. Last night had been euphoric until the point when she'd shared a kiss with Braden. She'd actually lost sleep over it because her stomach had been tied up in knots.

What had she been thinking by kissing him back? She should have pushed him away rather than melting into his embrace. And she'd ended up being totally embarrassed when he'd instantly regretted kissing her then told her he might be leaving Owl Creek. It had served as a one-two kick in the gut. This type of situation between them was unprecedented and incredibly awkward. If someone had told her last year that she and Braden would share a tender kiss in the future, Piper would have laughed them right out of town.

On several occasions Braden looked at her as if he wanted to say something. Each time Piper looked away and occupied herself with a task. She thought she might just scream if Braden brought it up. Right now even the slightest thing could push her over the edge.

Perhaps the Christmas countdown would help alleviate the tension. Today was ugly sweater day, and she was doing her best to honor the event by wearing the ugliest one she owned. In her opinion it was actually more adorable than ugly. Looking at the design reminded her of her father. Dancing penguins wearing Santa hats were emblazoned all over the fabric. Her parents had given it to her a long time ago, and she'd been wearing it every year since.

When she looked up from mopping up a coffee spill on the counter, Braden was standing in front of her, a quizzical expression stamped on his face.

"I was just wondering how long you plan to avoid me?" He tapped his watch. "We're already going on five hours now."

With a roll of her eyes, Piper responded, "Seriously, Braden. I have a lot on my mind with regards to the diner, so it's pretty self-absorbed of you to think you're the focus of my current mood."

Braden shrugged. "It's just that you've barely said two words to me all day. That's not normal." He plucked at his sweater. "And you didn't even comment on my Christmas lizards."

Piper looked up at the sweater. She honestly hadn't even noticed he was wearing it. She could feel the corners of her mouth twitching with merriment despite her vow to remain indifferent toward him. Braden had worn this particular sweater since high school, and it had generated loads of jokes between them. Just as she was about to make a funny comment about it, she remembered he was planning to leave her in the lurch all over again. A feeling of frustration stoked inside her. Why did it always seem as if she was being left behind? Even though she'd hoped things were mending between them, last night had put another wedge in their friendship. If he left Owl Creek, she wasn't sure their relationship would ever fully recover.

Piper shrugged. "Great sweater. I've got lots of work to do. These pies aren't going to bake themselves," she said.

"Piper—" Braden began before she cut him off.

"I've got to check in with Birdie and crunch some numbers. I need to see in black and white that they're shifting in a positive direction. If they're not, I might as well pack up and call it a day." She turned away from him just as she felt the sting of tears pricking her eyes. Piper beat a fast path to the small office at the rear of the kitchen. The last thing she needed or wanted was for Braden and her employees to see her break down in tears. As the owner of the Snowy Owl, she needed to maintain a stiff upper lip and an air of professionalism.

For the next hour, Piper busied herself with a dozen things related to the running of the diner. Several customers sought her out to tell her how much fun they'd had at the restaurant's tree trimming party. A quick scan of the numbers verified a big increase in profit due to their special promotions. While she'd lain awake last night, Piper had been hit with a grand idea. The pies were an undisputed hit. Even though the holidays would be over and done with in a few weeks, she needed to keep her eyes on maintaining a profit and not backsliding. Braden had been right. She needed to focus on the pies and become more entrepreneurial.

Pie in the Sky Pies. She would turn her pies into an actual business operating out of the Snowy Owl. Hadn't her father always dreamed of coming up with an idea that could increase his business and heighten the establishment's profile? She could start small and then build if sales justified it. And if it didn't take off, there wouldn't be a huge deficit. She would allow the pie business to grow organically and not take any major risks. Just thinking about this venture caused butterflies to soar around in her stomach. For the last four years, she'd been operating in the darkness without any foreseeable way out of the financial dilemma at the diner. Now, there was an opportunity to piggyback on the success of the pies and make a lasting impact.

Piper had a whole row of pies cooling on the counter while Clara and Jorge serviced the lunch orders. The increase in customers was sure and steady. Seeing all of the ugly sweaters served to uplift her. Everyone wanted to enter the ugly sweater contest in the hopes of winning the grand prize—a weekend at Trudy's inn along with dinner at the Snowy Owl and afternoon tea at Tea Time.

Braden entered the kitchen and approached her. "This has gone on for too long. Can we talk now?" he asked in a frustrated tone.

"I can't. Don't you see I'm baking at the moment?"

She let out a little squeal as Braden grabbed her

by the hand and began pulling her toward the door. She began flailing around. "What are you doing?"

"I need to talk to you in private. And since you're not speaking to me at the moment, you leave me no other choice." Braden led her outside through the back door despite her vocal resistance.

She wrapped her arms around her middle and faced him. "It's freezing out here! We could have gone into the back office to talk."

Braden spread his arms wide and looked up at the sky. "Why stay indoors when you have a great big Alaskan sky with the promise of snow at any moment?"

Piper quirked her mouth. "In case you haven't noticed, we already have enough snow on the ground to last till next Christmas. We hardly need any more."

"Snow is part of the Alaskan culture. Embrace it." Braden held out her coat, which she quickly shrugged into. "I want to show you something. It's going to turn that frown upside down."

She let out an exasperated groan. "Braden! I don't have time for show-and-tell. We actually have an increase in customers today, so it's all hands on deck. Plus I have to bake some more pies."

He grinned at her. "I can't dispute that those things are important, but you'll definitely want to make time for this. Give me ten minutes and I promise you won't regret it."

She clenched her jaw. How had she forgotten how persistent Braden could be when he became fixated on something? "Will you stop pestering me if I agree?"

"Yes. I promise. And don't worry about the diner. I already told the staff you were stepping out for a bit."

"I guess you thought of everything," she grumbled.

Undeterred by her snarky attitude, Braden motioned her to follow him as he began walking down Main Street. As she trailed after him, all Piper could think about was balancing the books and all the ingredients she needed to purchase in order to make more pies tomorrow. It was a never-ending cycle of work.

When Braden finally stopped walking, they were standing in front of Best Friends, a small veterinary practice with a lot of heart and expertly trained staff. Braden's lips were upturned in a mysterious smile as he opened the door wide so she could step in first. Owned by Vance Roberts, the clinic had been around for as long as Piper could remember. Vance's daughter, Maya, had recently returned to Owl Creek in order to help him run the practice after graduating from veterinary school.

A feeling of warmth surrounded her as soon as she stepped inside. Dogs were everywhere in the waiting room as they sat with their owners or playfully interacted with other canines.

"Hey there, guys." Maya greeted them warmly as they entered the vet practice. With her warm brown skin and auburn hair, she was a striking young woman who was celebrated all over town for her skill with animals. She was standing at the front desk holding a miniature poodle in her arms. "I have a feeling I know why you're here, Braden. Let me just put Copper in the exam room with my dad and I'll be right back."

"At least one of us knows," Piper said, shooting Braden a pointed look. As Maya walked away, she turned toward him. "What are we doing here?"

He stuffed his hands in his front pockets and rocked back on his heels. "I want you to meet someone."

"Meet someone? You dragged me out of the diner to introduce me to someone?" She knew her exasperation was on full display, but she was past caring. Braden was the most exasperating, confusing man on the planet. He was acting as if he didn't have a care in the world while she was losing sleep fretting about the diner's—and their friendship's—future.

"Here he is." Maya's cheery voice rang out as she walked toward the waiting room with a sweet Siberian husky at her side. The pup couldn't have been more than six months old. His gray-and-white coloring and blue eyes lent him a distinctive look.

"Hey there, boy," Braden crooned as he got down on his knees and greeted the dog with a warm hug. The husky responded by vigorously licking Braden's cheek.

"Oh, he's amazing!" Piper said, leaning over and rubbing his fur.

"You always said you wanted a Siberian husky," Braden added in a low voice. "He's a rescue dog. This could be your chance."

Braden was right. She was gazing upon her dream

dog. How many times had she talked about owning one with Braden? After their family dog, Blue, passed away, Piper had begged her parents to get another dog, but they'd been resistant. "I can never replace Blue," her father had always said. After Jack's death, Piper had let that fervent wish slip through her fingers. She'd been too grief-stricken to think about owning a dog. Maybe now she was ready to take that step.

"Piper, this is Rudolph," Maya said. "He's a rescue up for adoption. We've been calling him Rudy for short."

"Like Rudolph the red-nosed reindeer?" Piper asked, tickled by the idea of a Siberian husky being named after a beloved Christmas character from her favorite television movie.

Piper got down on her knees so she could be face-to-face with the pup. Somehow, even when she was furious with Braden, he managed to make her smile. He knew her better than she knew herself sometimes. "Hey there, cutie. I've been dreaming about you since I was a kid," she said, nuzzling her face against the Siberian husky. He responded by enthusiastically licking her face, toppling her over in the process.

"He seems to like you," Maya said. "Which doesn't surprise me one little bit. Dogs are great judges of character."

"I knew it! It's a perfect fit," Braden said, reaching out and patting Rudy on the head.

No matter how much she wanted to adopt Rudy, Piper didn't see it as feasible. It wouldn't be fair to the puppy to have an owner who was unavailable for such long periods of time. "But I'm at the diner all day," she said, letting out a groan. "It wouldn't be right to have him cooped up all day."

"He won't be a puppy for long. Then you can bring him to work with you. He could take naps in your office. Every business needs a mascot."

Piper knew it was true. Her father had always brought their dog, Blue, to the diner with him throughout the dog's life. But would she be assuming a responsibility greater than she could manage? Things in her life were already complicated enough. The timing was off with this very adorable dog. Although she knew Braden's heart had been in the right place by bringing her here to see Rudy, it broke her heart a little not to be able to say yes.

"Maybe you could take him, Braden. It might make more sense."

Braden shook his head. A sad expression passed over his face. "I can't."

Just as she was about to ask him why, it dawned on her, leaving her struggling with angry feelings all over again. "I get it. You can't take Rudy yourself because you don't plan to stick around town. Isn't that right?"

Braden didn't need to say a word. The truth was stamped all over his handsome face.

Maya's gaze darted back and forth between them. "I'll give the two of you a few minutes," she said before quietly removing herself from the tension-filled situation.

Piper jumped to her feet and brushed her hands off

on her pants. It was just like Braden to dangle something in front of her eyes that was out of her reach. He wasn't always a practical person. He did things on the spur of the moment, which had always been endearing until recently. Tears of frustration filled her eyes. She really needed to be at the diner working right now. And instead, Braden had led her on a wild-goose chase that hadn't amounted to anything more than exasperation. She leaned down and patted the husky's fur. "It was nice meeting you, Rudy. I hope you find an awesome home. I wish it could be with me."

With a shake of her head in Braden's direction, Piper turned on her heel and walked out of the veterinary clinic. She ducked her chin against the cold wind blowing in her direction. She knew on some level that Braden had been trying to do something nice for her, but this excursion had only served as a reminder that her best friend's presence in town was temporary. When he had left before, Piper had learned the hard way how much she'd always depended on him. It had felt like she'd been missing her right arm without him.

And now, just as she'd gotten used to Braden being back home, there was a strong possibility he might leave her all over again. Piper knew it would be just as excruciating as the first time. Before he could break her heart all over again, she vowed to distance herself from him. It would be the only surefire way to ensure that she wouldn't fall apart at the seams if and when he decided to leave.

Chapter Ten

"I don't have time for Christmas caroling tonight, Mama," Piper said. "I'm too busy with the Snowy Owl."

Braden could hear the longing in Piper's voice. She was making practical decisions even though her heart was leading her elsewhere. He knew how much she loved singing and being a part of the Owl Creek community.

"Piper, it's the holidays. You have to make time for things that replenish your soul," Trudy chided. "Isn't that right, Braden?" Although he'd been within earshot of the conversation between Piper and her mother, Braden hadn't wanted it to appear as if he was eavesdropping. He was still walking on eggshells with Piper. He'd come over early to the diner so he could help her open up the restaurant and set up the tables. Although refilling salt and pepper shakers wasn't his heart's desire, there wasn't anything he wouldn't do to help Piper succeed with the diner.

Taking her to meet Rudy the other day hadn't been the smartest move. His heart had been in the right place, but he'd made a mess of things. Piper loved dogs, and he'd mistakenly thought she would jump at the opportunity to bring Rudy home. All it had done was shine a light on the fact that he might not be sticking around Owl Creek. Although Piper was talking to him, she wasn't being warm and fuzzy. She wasn't acting like herself. He missed his best friend.

At the moment both Piper and Trudy were looking in his direction, awaiting his answer.

"The holidays are definitely a time to spread holiday cheer and take a little time to be with family and friends, but business has increased tenfold since the holiday stroll so Piper needs to capitalize on it," he said, being careful not to allude to the diner's financial problems. It was tricky since Piper still hadn't told her mother about the urgent need to turn things around. That was frustrating because if Trudy knew about the diner's woes, she would understand her daughter's need to bypass some of the holiday celebrations in favor of working.

"And with Jorge needed elsewhere at the moment," Piper added, "I really must stick close to the diner."

Piper had received the call from her employee late last night informing her that his wife, Irina, had gone into labor. Hours later he'd announced that they were the proud parents of an eight-pound baby boy named Charlie. They were all doing well and feeling grateful for their little Christmas blessing. Jorge would be enjoying a family leave of absence for at least a week.

"That's such wonderful news for their family," Trudy crowed. "Your father adored Jorge. He'd be so tickled with all the wonderful things happening in his life. A wife and now a baby boy."

"He would be," Piper agreed. "Everyone who worked at the diner was considered family. They still are. That's what made the Snowy Owl so special."

"I can hang around tonight and provide coverage if you want to go caroling," Braden offered. "Between me and the staff, we can cover for you. You deserve a night off after all the hard work you've put in over the last four years."

A sigh slipped past her lips. "Thanks for the offer, but it's best I stick around. We're short-staffed as it is, and I'm hoping we get a big crowd tonight. I'm the face of the Snowy Owl, so I should be here greeting the customers."

"Well, thank you for the pies," Trudy said, picking up the brown paper bag that held two of the sought after baked goods. "It's nice to have an in with the owner. My guests will be delighted. Everyone is buzzing about them."

Piper grinned. "See you later, Mama. Have fun tonight," she called out after her as she exited the diner.

Braden looked at his watch. It was almost time to open up the place. Piper was sitting at the counter scribbling in a notebook. She was staring at the page intently while nibbling at the end of her pencil.

She seemed to be in a completely different world at the moment.

"What do you have there?" he asked, curious about her being so engrossed in something other than the Snowy Owl.

She looked up at him with a startled expression. He could tell she'd been deep in thought about something. "I'm just making some notes. I've been thinking over a few things. It might be crazy to go all out like this, but I came up with an idea to expand the pies into an actual business."

"A business?" he asked, surprised by Piper's statement.

She held up her hand. "I know it's ambitious, but the pies have taken the town by storm. Along with the milkshakes, they're really making a big difference to the diner's bottom line. I was looking at the numbers, and it hit me that if we—" She stopped speaking abruptly.

"Go on," he urged. "If we do what?"

"I shouldn't really say 'we,' Braden. You could be leaving Owl Creek soon. I can't really count on you to be a part of the team, even though you were the one who put me on this road in the first place." They locked gazes. He could see the raw emotion emanating from her eyes. Something powerful crackled in the air. It terrified him because he knew his pulse shouldn't be racing, and he shouldn't feel like his heart was being squeezed by a giant fist. It stunned him to the point where he couldn't even find the words to comfort his best friend.

He didn't know yet whether he was going to leave or stay. It would be cruel to make promises he might not be able to keep. It would be like ripping a rug out from underneath her feet. In his heart he yearned to stay in his hometown even though it seemed as if he couldn't do right by Piper no matter how hard he tried. But maybe he should stick around and try. If he really wanted to achieve redemption, running away wasn't an option.

"I'm grateful, Braden. Without you I probably would have just given up and thrown in the towel. I know things have been strained between us, but you really stepped up to help me. Because of you I started brainstorming ideas to bring more income to the diner."

"That's all you," Braden responded. "It's who you are, Piper. A go-getter. You've always been the type of person who wants to make things better. You were just afraid of losing your dad's establishment so you got stuck. That's a lot of pressure on one person's shoulders. If I helped in any way, that makes me happy, but you're the driving force behind the diner, as well as being its future. So tell me more about your idea."

Piper's grin made his stomach do belly flops. Happiness looked good on her. "Okay, so don't laugh but I came up with a name." She waited a moment before speaking. "Pie in the Sky. That's the name I want to give the new venture. I want to start really small because I know it's not going to be easy, but my goal is to increase revenue and to do something

I really love, which is making pies." She inhaled a deep breath. "Am I babbling? Because I really feel like I'm talking way too fast from nerves. Tell me what you think."

Pie in the Sky. It was clever and spot-on. He nodded, appreciating Piper's vision. "I love the name. It fits with the whole idea of how it came about. Are you planning to stay local or branch out?"

"Definitely local. I want the townsfolk to think of it as fresh, flavorful pies sold out of the Snowy Owl. But if things take off, perhaps I can open up a small shop next door. I don't want to get ahead of myself, but at the moment people seem to want whole pies rather than slices, which is more lucrative for me."

"Starting small is a good idea just to make sure you're not getting into a situation that's over your head. How do you plan to officially launch it? And what about money? Investors? There are going to be costs associated with it."

Piper shrugged. "I don't have all the answers yet. But I'd like to have a soft launch right before Christmas. No bells and whistles. Just letting the townsfolk know that the pies are here to stay, and we'll be taking orders under the new name—Pie in the Sky."

Braden rubbed his hands together. "I like the idea of a soft launch. There really won't be a lot of pressure since you're already taking pie orders."

Just then the front door rattled, alerting them to the fact that they'd been so deep in conversation that the front door was still locked. Elena came from the kitchen and made her way to the front, quickly placing an Open sign on the door.

"I feel so blessed to have such hardworking and loyal workers," Piper said, watching Elena ushering guests inside. "I'd be lost without them."

"People tend to give back what they get," Braden said. "You make everyone feel like family, just like Jack did."

A smile played around Piper's lips. "Pie in the Sky talk to be continued," she said to Braden, standing up and shoving her notebook under her arm before heading behind the counter.

Braden's eyes trailed after Piper. He liked seeing her upbeat and optimistic. A part of him wanted to stick around Owl Creek simply so he could be a part of the launch of Pie in the Sky. It was exciting seeing Piper's creativity in action. Things were looking up for her and the Snowy Owl Diner. He wanted to watch it all come to fruition. Wasn't that the role of a best friend?

Perhaps then his guilt wouldn't be swallowing him up whole. Maybe he would find peace with the situation. And with himself.

Lately, he'd been all over the place. About his past, present and future. Piper had always been his best friend, yet he felt stirrings of something else that confused him. He couldn't deny he felt a pull in her direction that seemed different from anything he'd experienced with her up to this point. Perhaps it was tied up in his guilt. Or his deep sense of remorse. Keeping secrets weighed on a person in a manner he'd never really understood until now. He knew enough to realize he could never truly be free unless he unburdened himself of everything weighing him down. If only he could summon the courage and see it through.

The strange vibe brewing between him and Piper confused him. He had a hard time wrapping his head around anything romantic going on. Piper had always been his best friend. Anything more between them was simply out of the question.

Piper hadn't expected for Braden to be so enthusiastic about Pie in the Sky. All day she'd been upbeat just thinking about the future. Braden's support meant the world to her. It made her believe she could really put Pie in the Sky in motion. And with the additional income, she could try to dig her way out of the financial hole she was in. Maybe she wouldn't have to close the diner's doors. Her heart wouldn't be broken over failing to save it. She could actually feel proud of her efforts.

If she was being honest with herself, perhaps she'd been waiting for Braden to talk her out of moving forward with her new venture. It was a bit terrifying to put herself out there in such a grand way. What if the pie business didn't take off? It would be embarrassing to fall on her face. What if she needed to put a lot of cash into the enterprise? She would start small and keep building on it. Baby steps. It wasn't as if the Norths had built up their chocolate empire overnight.

Even though she didn't have all of the answers, it sure felt good to feel hopeful. Isn't that what Christmas was all about? Faith? The hope of something wonderful just around the corner.

"What's that noise?" Piper asked as a loud rhythmic sound emanated from outside.

Braden had a huge smile on his face. "I think I know."

She rushed toward the door and yanked it open. A large group of carolers, with her mother right in the center, were walking up the stairs and toward the front door. Piper stepped aside to let them by. As the carolers headed inside, they continued to sing "Silent Night." Their charming melody rang out sweetly in the diner as customers stopped eating to listen to their Christmas carols.

Among the group was Hank, his daughter, Addie, and Sage. Piper plucked Addie from Hank's arms and pressed a kiss on the toddler's cheek. She stayed in Piper's arms for a few minutes until she reached out for Sage. It made Piper happy to see her niece bonding so well with her sister-in-law. In marrying Hank, Sage had given Addie a new mother. Her own mother had died in a car accident when she was a few months old. Watching their loving family caused a feeling of envy to rise up inside her. It must be nice, she thought, to have a soft place to fall when the world crashed in around you.

In many ways Braden served that role in her life. It was the reason she was so upset about not having him around in the future. She'd gotten so accustomed to having him back in her life that it was near impossible to imagine her world without him in it. Even when things were tense between them or when they were angry at one another, their connection still persisted. Bent but not broken.

The carolers sang a medley of Christmas songs, their voices blended together in perfect harmony. At the end of the performance, all of the customers in the diner stood up and cheered. It had added a special dose of holiday cheer to the evening. It was moments like this one that made the season so uplifting and enjoyable. Singing was a gift, and tonight it had been shared with so many residents of Owl Creek. Despite all the ups and downs of the past weeks and months, Piper felt inspired.

"Thank you so much for thinking of us. Hot cocoa coming up for everyone!" Piper called out. "And we have fresh cider doughnuts on the counter for everyone to enjoy."

All of the carolers cheered and made their way over to the counter where Braden and some other staff members were ladling hot chocolate into foam cups. Piper walked over and hugged her mother tightly. "Mama! Thank you for bringing the carolers right to my doorstep. What a wonderful gift."

"I can't take the credit. It was Braden's idea," Trudy said. "He thought you could use a big dose of holiday cheer." Trudy grinned. "He's going to make some woman a fine husband one day."

"He sure will," Piper murmured, trying to ignore the little ache that particular knowledge caused her.

It was hard to even envision Braden settling down with his other half and raising a house full of children. As a kid, he had always said he never wanted to get married, but Piper had always pictured him with a family.

She wasn't sure if she was imagining the pointed look her mother gave her. Perhaps she was just being paranoid after the tender kiss they'd shared. More than anyone, her mother knew she and Braden were simply friends.

A quick gaze around the room showed Braden talking to his grandparents who were also part of the caroling group. His head was thrown back in merriment, showcasing his congenial personality and good looks. She couldn't even tell herself it wouldn't hurt when Braden fell in love and paired off with someone. It would no doubt signal a vast change in their friendship. Perhaps this whole time she'd been resisting the inevitable adjustments that came with adulthood. Maybe the tension between them was nothing more than growing pains. It didn't make it hurt any less.

"Thanks for the hot cocoa," Hank said as he came up beside her and lifted his cup in the air. "It's perfect after being outside in the cold." He shivered, drawing laughter from Piper.

"Sure thing," she said. "It's the least I could do after the wonderful performance we were treated to. You guys are terrific. I hated to miss it, so this was really special."

"I think so too," Sage said, walking up and joining them. She looped her arm through Hank's as she juggled Addie on her hip. "There's nothing quite like an Owl Creek Christmas."

"A bit different from Florida, huh?" Piper asked. Up until this past year, Sage had been a Floridian, so acclimating to the Alaskan way of life had been a bit daunting at first. Now, it seemed as if she had always been a member of their community.

"You have no idea," Sage said, garnering laughter from the group.

Suddenly, Beulah strode over with Jennings at her side. "We should get back out there, carolers. It's getting late," she said in a raised voice. "And the temperature will be dipping to uncomfortable levels in an hour or so."

Everyone in town knew Beulah as being a no-nonsense and direct person. She said things very decisively and left no room for argument. She'd led the carolers for as long as Piper could remember. Once Beulah made her announcement, all of the singers immediately began to head toward the door, calling out holiday wishes and blessings as they left. Piper and Braden trailed after them, waving and thanking the group for stopping by. They were standing so close in the doorway that their arms were touching. Piper resisted the impulse to loop her arm through his as she might have done before things had gotten strained between them. The lines between them were becoming blurred, and it was both surprising and terrifying. She didn't want to do a single thing to add to the strange tension pulsing between them. Touching Braden felt a little bit off-limits.

It frustrated her to have to second-guess every move and gesture. Best friends shouldn't have to worry about things like this. She wished she could be transported back in time to the days when everything between them had been effortless.

As they turned to head into the diner, Piper stumbled on the top step. Braden reached out to save her from falling and quickly pulled her against his chest. Instinctively, Piper raised both of her hands against his body in order to catch herself. Braden's chest was like a sheet of iron, with an abundance of muscles. She looked up at him, sucking in a deep, steadying breath at the sudden physical contact between them. Her hands seemed clumsy.

"Are you all right?" he asked, worry imprinted on his face.

Piper nodded. Her throat felt thick and heavy. She didn't trust herself to speak at the moment. Although she'd tried to dismiss it before, once again something electric was humming and pulsing in the air around them.

Braden was looking down at her with surprise radiating from his eyes. She took a step backward, wanting to distance herself from this unsettling reality. She couldn't pretend anymore that things hadn't shifted between her and Braden. Surely he must be aware of it too even though he'd brushed it off after the tender kiss they'd shared. Perhaps it had been his way of coping with something neither one of them seemed ready to face head-on.

"I—I better get back to the kitchen and check in

with Clara," she said in a low voice, interrupting the silence.

She practically scampered inside, desperate to get back to running the diner rather than experiencing uncomfortable moments with a person who'd always felt like family. Piper didn't bother to turn around to see if Braden had come back inside. She didn't trust herself to even look at him. It felt risky. For so long now she'd been telling herself to focus on saving the diner. But lately, her attention had been diverted by all her issues with Braden. She'd tossed and turned a few nights just thinking about the distance between them. And now she found herself worrying about the moments where it seemed as if an attraction was brewing between them.

He was important to her—in some ways now more than ever. Braden had stepped in to help her rescue her family's business from financial ruin when she had no one else to rely on. He was the closest thing to a hero she'd ever known. She cared about him more than almost anyone else in her life, except for Mama and Hank.

She couldn't help but worry that she was going to lose her best friend, and there was nothing she could do to stop it from happening.

"Let me stay and help you lock up," Braden offered as the last customers straggled out and Clara and the wait staff bid them good-night.

"Honestly, I'm so tired I can't even pretend not to need the help. I may need to get a better pair of shoes," Piper said, her shoulders slumping. "I'd love a cup of coffee, but I'm afraid it would keep me up all night."

"You need to go home and get a good night's rest. Maybe soak your feet in a footbath. You've really been pushing yourself to the point of exhaustion. You need to take a day off to rejuvenate."

Piper raised a hand to her mouth in mock surprise. "A day off? What's that?" she cracked. "I can't remember the last time I took off work."

"I'm glad you're training Jorge to have more responsibilities, because you need someone who can serve as a backup. What happens if you're sick or want to go on vacation?"

Piper let out a brittle sounding laugh. "Vacation? The last one I had was a day trip to Homer. Hank subbed for me that day if I remember correctly. He grew up in the diner so he knows it inside and out. I trust him completely."

"I'm happy he could be there for you, but Hank is town sheriff. He has his own full-time job, as does your mother. You need someone on staff who can lighten the load off your shoulders."

She let out a ragged sigh. "I know. There's got to be a better way. And once I get over this hurdle, I'm going to fix those staffing holes, starting with promoting Jorge."

"It'll make your life easier," Braden said. He reached out and ran his finger across her forehead. "I don't like these little worry lines here. I'd rather see laugh lines on your face."

Braden's cell phone began to buzz insistently. He looked down at the screen. He'd been waiting for this call all evening. Now that he'd decided to stay in Owl Creek he was going to move forward with rebuilding his life here. "I need to answer this," he told Piper before moving a few feet away. "Hey there, Maya. I can meet you outside the diner in a few minutes. Just locking up the place now. Okay. See you in a few."

Seconds later he hung up and pulled his coat on, eager to meet Maya. Piper already had her coat, hat and boots on, clearly ready to call it a night. He walked out with Piper, pausing as she locked the door and placed the Closed sign on it. Light snow was beginning to fall from the sky, although it didn't appear to be sticking on the ground. Braden stopped at the bottom of the stairs as he spotted Maya walking toward them with Rudy by her side.

"Here's your very special delivery," Maya said as she reached them, handing over the leash to Braden.

He grinned at the sight of the Siberian husky. He bent over and slapped at his knees, beckoning Rudy to his side. In response, the puppy began to wag his tail and lick Braden's hands.

"What's going on?" Piper asked. She was looking at him suspiciously.

"I figured since Rudy needs a good home and I love dogs more than I do people, I would be a great candidate for adopting him since you can't."

Piper's mouth hung open. "You're adopting Rudy?"

"He is." Maya confirmed with a grin. "I have a

bag of treats and dog food you can pick up tomorrow." She handed him a small bag. "This is enough until the morning. You can swing by the practice at your leisure to get the rest of his stuff."

"Thanks for everything," Braden said, leaning in to give Maya a hug. "I promise I'll do right by him."

"I have no doubts about that, Braden. Merry Christmas," she said before walking back toward the vet clinic.

"Happy holidays!" Braden called out in unison with Piper, who couldn't seem to take her eyes off the Siberian husky. She was kneeling down beside him, talking to Rudy in a sweet tone. Her love for dogs was as great as his own. Her expression was one of pure wonder.

She looked up at him. "I can't believe you're taking Rudy home with you."

Braden shoved his hands in his pockets. "Well, he really needed a home and since you couldn't take him, I decided it should be me. Rudy and I were buddies from the moment we met. As a result, he's the newest member of the North family."

"Who's going to take care of him during the day?" Piper asked, wrinkling her nose as the dog licked her face. She let out a little squeal of delight.

"My grandfather has already agreed to do it. And Rudy's housebroken so it shouldn't be a hardship."

"So, does this mean you're sticking around Owl Creek?" she asked, a hopeful expression etched on her face.

Braden paused a moment before answering. He'd

faced the fact that running wasn't the answer. He had already done it once, and it hadn't helped him or anyone else. If he truly wanted to move forward, he needed to stick around town and face the music.

He felt a smile tugging at his lips. "Yes, I'm staying. I came to the conclusion that I need to be here in Owl Creek," he admitted. "Traveling all over the world is overrated, plus I think my remaining in town would be the best Christmas present for my family. It's been a long time since we've all been together like this."

"It will be a great present for me, as well," Piper told him. Braden wasn't prepared for Piper to wrap him in a hug and press her head against his chest. It was wonderful to have her in his arms, especially when half the time they seemed to be at odds. Holding her made him feel as if he could protect her from anything in the world that might cause her pain, even the secret he was keeping.

"Look! Northern lights!" Braden called out as the sky exploded in a stunning, shimmery display of beauty. It was such a spectacular sight one never got tired of. A burst of brilliant colors lit up the night sky. Reds. Greens. Vibrant purples and blues. He heard Piper's sharp exclamation of surprise. Her face was upturned, and for the life of him he couldn't figure out whether to look at her or the northern lights. If he had to choose, he'd pick Piper each and every time.

"What a magnificent surprise." Piper's eyes were wide with wonder. For a moment he was reminded of the little girl she'd once been. Piper had always been full of enthusiasm and a positive outlook. He felt thankful that her spirit of optimism hadn't been stamped out by the death of her father and her on-going troubles with the diner. She'd walked a tough road over the past few years, and she still continued to shine. She didn't hesitate to embrace joy.

"One of Alaska's many marvels," Braden said. "Of all the places I've been, nothing compares to the last frontier. Nowhere even comes close." He'd trav-eled the world, and his heart still belonged to Alaska. Nothing could compare to the harsh, rugged land of his birth and Alaskan way of life. It served as a huge incentive to stay put.

"This has been a spectacular night. Between the carolers and the northern lights, I feel so incredibly blessed."

"I always have fun when I'm with you, Piper. We could be washing dishes in the kitchen or skipping stones across the lake for all I care. It's being with you that makes it special. I want you to know that."

"Thank you for saying so. I've missed us. You have no idea how many nights I laid awake wonder-ing where you were in the world and what you were up to. I imagined you were doing incredible things and that you'd forgotten all about Owl Creek."

"I could never forget this town or you. Not a day went by when I didn't think about what I'd left be-hind. Some days I was so homesick I wanted to come right back."

"Then why didn't you? There was a tremendous void in Owl Creek when you left." Hurt radiated from her eyes. He hated being the one who'd made her feel this way.

Maybe he could tell her the truth right here and now. Perhaps then she would understand why he'd stayed away from Alaska for such a long time. Maybe she wouldn't hate him as he'd always feared. Was it possible she might show him a measure of compassion?

"Because I had some growing to do," he answered. "And I couldn't do it here. Sometimes you have to leave a place to become the person you want to be."

"And did you?" she asked pointedly.

He shook his head. "Not even close," he admitted. It was hard to become a better man when he was keeping secrets and living in fear of being found out. But he couldn't explain any of that to Piper, even though he really wanted to.

"You're being hard on yourself, Braden. I think you're a pretty amazing human being." She was gazing up at him, and for the first time in a long time, the expression emanating from her eyes was one of absolute confidence in him. He wasn't sure he deserved it, but it made him feel good knowing she still believed in him. Especially when most days he had a hard time having faith in himself.

Being here with Piper with snow falling all around them and his gorgeous new dog lying at his feet made Braden feel as if all was right in his world. Just for a little bit he could pretend he wasn't standing on a crumbling foundation. He wanted to relish this moment because he knew it was temporary.

Braden knew it wasn't smart to consider kissing Piper again, but he was tired of being ruled by his head instead of his heart. Sometimes a person just had to step out on a limb of faith and act without overthinking it. Moments like this didn't come around very often. He pulled Piper close, then leaned down and pressed his lips against hers in a tender, romantic kiss that was just as spectacular as the first one. Piper's scent filled his nostrils—a light, floral aroma. Her lips tasted like hot cocoa and cinnamon.

When the kiss ended, neither one said a word. They both seemed to be enjoying the quiet that enveloped them. Their relationship had always been full of companionable silences where neither one felt the need to fill it up with mindless chatter. His fingers trailed through her curls as they settled into the silence. It had been a fantastic kiss, Braden realized. One for the record books, if he was being honest. Tender and full of emotion. It had been the furthest thing from run-of-the-mill. That knowledge hit him in the face like a sledgehammer.

"You kissed me. Again," she said, raising her hand to touch her lips.

"I did, didn't I?" Braden said, smiling down at her. He didn't feel regretful or as if he was going to hang his head in shame over the kiss. It had been sheer perfection. He couldn't even pretend he hadn't thoroughly enjoyed it.

Piper was gazing up at him with doubt pooling

in her eyes. "Last time you said our kiss was a mistake. You've never been the type of person to repeat your missteps."

Braden reached out to brush her wayward curls away from her forehead. He wanted to make sure he could see her eyes at this special moment. He wanted to savor it because he knew it wouldn't last once she found out his secret. Maybe it was selfish of him, but he'd kissed her knowing a huge chasm sat between them that could never be bridged.

"It wasn't even close to being a mistake, Piper. In fact, it might just have been the smartest thing I've ever done."

The smile that crept over Piper's face threatened to take over her entire face. "That's really nice to hear, especially after what you said last time. I have to admit it left me feeling pretty confused."

He shook his head. "I—I wasn't trying to hurt you. Matter of fact, I was trying not to further complicate things between us since I thought I was going to leave after Christmas."

"Now that you're not leaving, have you told your family you don't want to work at the family business? If not, you really should," she said, her brows knit together. "The sooner you tell them the better."

He ran a hand over his face. "I've been dragging my feet about doing it, but you're right. I'm supposed to be starting after the holidays are over."

She squeezed his arm. "They'll understand, Braden. As long as you speak from the heart and tell them exactly how you feel, your family will accept it. They love you."

He let out a low chuckle. "When did you become such a fount of wisdom?" he asked.

Piper scoffed. "Trust me, I don't have all the answers. If I did, I would have patched up all the problems with the diner a long time ago." Her smile hit him squarely in his solar plexus. Had she always been this stunning? These days it seemed as if he was seeing her through a completely different lens. And he liked what he was seeing!

"You're beautiful, Piper. You always have been, but ever since I came back it's hard for me to remember you used to be a knock-kneed tomboy."

Piper let out a sound of outrage. "Knock-kneed? Those are fighting words, Braden North. I wasn't any such thing and you know it."

Braden threw his head back in laughter. He'd said the word on purpose, knowing it would get a heated response from her.

"Take it back!" she demanded, playfully shoving against his chest.

"Okay, I will. I was just teasing," he admitted, holding up his hands in surrender. "You weren't even close to being knock-kneed. Matter of fact, you were always the prettiest girl in Owl Creek, bar none."

She shook her head. He wasn't sure if it was his comment or the cold air, but her cheeks were flushed and rosy. "I don't know about that, but you're really sweet for saying it."

He brushed his knuckles against her cheek. "It's

getting late. You need your rest, and I've got to take Rudy home."

"Good night, Braden." She bent down and ruffled Rudy's fur. "Night, Rudy."

Braden stood by her truck as she got in and started the engine. He stood by for a few minutes until Piper warmed it up a little then drove off into the night.

"Ready to go home, boy?" he asked Rudy as he opened the passenger door of his truck and prompted the dog to jump in. Braden got behind the wheel and let out a throaty chuckle as he turned to look at Rudy. He was making himself comfortable in the seat. As he drove home, Braden let out a sigh. As Piper had stated earlier, it had been a fantastic day full of unexpected surprises. Now that he had decided to stay in Owl Creek, Braden knew he had to figure out a plan for his future. His secret was still sitting between him and Piper. He had to work out how to tell her and deal with the consequences if she decided not to forgive him. And if North Star Chocolates wasn't going to be his vocation, it was important to find something else that would pay the bills. He wanted to show his family that he wasn't simply slacking by declining their job offer.

Now, he just had to decide how to make a living while still pursuing his love of adventure, the great outdoors and sports. He'd been doing a lot of brainstorming. It might not be easy to pull it off, but he was determined to make it happen. His family had made Owl Creek a tourist attraction due to their chocolate factory. Could he capitalize on the tourism aspect and create something of his very own? Piper had inspired him to hold fast to his dreams.

If she could turn things around at the Snowy Owl, then Braden could also reach out for what he wanted most. One way or another, he was determined to live out his dreams right here in Owl Creek.

Chapter Eleven

Braden stood by the large Christmas tree in the great room of the family home, admiring the festive decorations his mother had put up with so much love and care. He smiled at the sight of all the red-and-white stockings hanging from the stone mantelpiece. There really was no place like home. The large bay window provided a bird's-eye view of his family's property. Snow covered the ground, courtesy of a fast-moving storm that had blanketed Owl Creek last evening. He let out a deep sigh and gazed at the snowcapped mountains in the distance. Nothing made him feel more at peace than the sight of the Alaskan vista.

Even from this distance he could sometimes see owls soaring over the woods at dawn. A pine tree fully decorated in ornaments, mini lights and tinsel sat near the driveway. At night its multicolored lights shimmered and winked from outside, providing a festive air to the North family home. Despite his knee-jerk decision to leave town after Jack's death, he knew with a deep certainty there was no finer place than this town he loved so dearly.

He needed to be courageous in all things. Above all else, he needed to come clean with Piper and tell her the truth. Only then would he be able to move toward the life he so wanted to live here in Owl Creek. Braden knew without a doubt that he'd put off his talk with Connor long enough. Since he wasn't expected at the diner until later on this morning, he figured there was no time like the present. His brother was in the kitchen rumbling around making himself some breakfast. If he caught him before he left for the office, they could have some quality time to talk things over.

Give me courage, he prayed. Although he and Connor were both adults, he still felt as if his older brother was wiser and more measured than he could ever hope to be. Braden admired and respected him more than he could ever express in words.

When he walked into the kitchen, Connor was sitting down at the table eating a big bowl of oatmeal mixed with berries. A tall glass of orange juice sat beside his plate.

"Morning," Connor said with a nod. "Surprised to see you here. You've been going to the diner pretty early every morning. Our paths hardly ever cross."

"Good morning. I'm heading in a little bit later." He cuffed the back of his neck. "Can we talk? There's something I need to tell you."

"Sure thing. What's going on?" he asked, placing

his spoon down and motioning for Braden to join him at the table.

Braden sat down across from his brother. He fiddled nervously with his fingers. "I'm not coming to work at North Star Chocolates."

"You're what?" Connor asked, leaning forward in his seat. "I don't think that I heard you right."

"I've decided not to become a junior executive at the company." In response to his statement, Connor's mouth went slack.

"You're joking, right?" Connor stammered.

Braden met his brother's steady gaze from across the table. "I respect you too much to ever do that. I'm serious, Connor."

Connor ran a hand through his hair. "It's all we've ever talked about since we were kids. What happened to change your mind?" Connor's expression gutted Braden. He appeared crestfallen by the news. It packed an extra punch since his older brother rarely showed his emotional side. Ever since they were little, Connor had been the stoic one. He prayed his brother would understand and not feel betrayed by his decision. He was one of the most important people in his life, and he treasured their brotherly bond.

"Where do I start?" Braden let out a ragged sigh. "It's not where my heart lies at the moment. I love North Star Chocolates and the legacy our family has created. It gives me an immeasurable sense of pride to even be affiliated with it, but I can't imagine I'd be happy stuck behind a desk all day. I'm just not that guy. I can't imagine I ever will be."

"Maybe we can work something out. It's not all drudgery. There's travel to Switzerland and Belgium to attend meetings and chocolatier conferences." Connor's expression brightened. His voice sounded hopeful. "You love to travel."

Braden crossed his hands in front of him. "I don't think so. I've spent the last three years running from things I haven't been able to face up to. I can't do that anymore. Now that our family is whole with Sage back in the fold, I have to commit myself to living my best life."

Connor sat back in his chair and folded his arms across his chest. Braden knew his brother was floored by the information he'd just dumped on him.

After a few moments, Connor said, "I get it, Braden. I'm sad we won't be working together, but I'm happy you're back here in our hometown. That means a lot to me. Having you back is the most important thing."

His shoulders sagged with relief. "Thanks, Connor. You've always been one of my biggest supporters."

"That won't ever change. I promise. So what do you see yourself doing?" He dipped his spoon back in his oatmeal and pushed a large amount into his mouth. "At least you have your trust fund to help you get something started."

Connor was right. Their grandparents had set up sizable trust funds for him, Connor and Sage. Although he'd used some of his money to travel all over the world for the past few years, he still had a considerable amount left, some of which he wanted to use to help support Pie in the Sky. Although Piper had frowned on accepting money to help her turn things around at the Snowy Owl, he was determined to become one of her investors. He wasn't going to take no for an answer. For now, it would be his secret.

He cupped his hands around his mug and took a swig of the sweet smelling hot chocolate. "I love the great outdoors and all of the adventures I've experienced over the last few years. But I also hate being away from the people I love here in Owl Creek, so I've got to figure out a way of merging all of those things into a career I can really be proud of. I want to go to work every day knowing I'm doing what my heart is calling me to do."

"If anyone can do it, you can. You've always had a knack for finding your way through the difficult times. You've got this."

Connor stood up and came around to Braden's side of the table. Braden stood up and the brothers hugged it out. When they pulled apart, Connor heartily clapped Braden on the back. "I need to head over to the factory. Now that I can't dump half the work on you, I'd better get to it," he teased. As Connor headed out of the kitchen, Braden let out a sigh of relief. He'd been so worried about his big brother's reaction to his decision, but like always, Connor had a way of surprising him by his compassion and understanding. It was part of what made him such an exceptional person.

Footsteps sounded behind him. When he turned

around, Beulah was standing a few feet away from him, a quizzical expression etched on her face. Dressed in her signature pearls, she was wearing a hunter green skirt and a black silk shirt. Her hair was perfectly coiffed as if she had just left a salon.

"So, when were you going to share the news with me?" Beulah asked, hands on her hips.

"Grandma. I didn't know you were still here. How much of our conversation did you hear?"

She frowned. "Enough to know what you've decided about your future at North Star Chocolates."

Braden's heart sank. He hated hurting his grandmother. Her dream had always been to bring the North family together to work for their chocolate empire. Even though Sage was a teacher, she still worked in a part-time capacity for North Star Chocolates. He would be the first one to veer away from the North family business. He hated being the one to break the chain.

"I'm sorry. I feel like I've come back home after all this time only to disappoint you."

Beulah crossed her arms over her chest and tapped her booted foot on the hardwood floor. "Who said you disappointed me? If there's one thing I hate, it's when people put words in my mouth. You're my grandson, Braden North. It's practically impossible for you to let me down."

Braden regarded her with a skeptical eye. "Even if I won't be working for North Star Chocolates?"

Beulah gifted him with a beatific smile. "Even if

you were to move to Tahiti and open up a surf shop, I'd still be your biggest fan."

Braden chuckled. "You know I don't know how to surf. Not sure I can even picture it." He winked at her. "I'm an Alaskan, through and through."

Beulah reached out and swept her palm across his cheek. "My point is…you're special to me, Braden. Always have been. Always will be. Family is everything. I'll always want you to be close by, but I care about your happiness, wherever it may lead you."

Braden leaned down and pressed a kiss on Beulah's temple. "It led me straight back to Owl Creek. It's exactly where I want to be."

"This town wasn't the same without you," she said, tears glistening in her eyes. "Just ask Piper. She walked around town like a shell of her former self after you left."

"Don't forget she was in mourning for her father," he explained. Once again guilt threatened to swallow him up whole. "I suppose my departure didn't help matters any."

"Now be honest. What's going on between you and Piper? And don't tell me it's simply friendship. I was born at night, but not last night." Beulah cocked her head to the side and studied him with a critical eye. "I watched the two of you in the diner after the caroling, and there was something simmering in the air between you. Are you falling for her?"

There was really no point in trying to hide anything from the town's biggest know-it-all. Of all people, he could never fool his grandmother. "I think it's safe to say I've already fallen. But we're just friends." Just saying the words out loud caused his pulse to skitter like crazy. It felt a little bit terrifying to admit how far gone he was. Although he thought Piper's feelings mirrored his own, he had no proof. Anyway, his secret could ruin everything.

"Have you told her?" Beulah pressed.

"Not in so many words," he admitted, instantly regretting being so candid. Beulah was known for being forceful. The very last thing he needed was to have her butting into his love life. "There's something important I need to tell her that I should have come clean about a long time ago."

"What are you waiting for? Time waits for no one. If you want to move forward with your life, it's important to get that off your chest. You're a North. Be bold like your grandfather was when he courted me."

"I agree," he said, realizing Beulah was never wrong. If he wanted a future with Piper, he needed to lay his heart bare. Staying in the friend zone would no longer do. "I just don't want to mess up our friendship. What if she doesn't reciprocate my feelings?"

"Trust your gut. And if you care one whit about my opinion, Piper thinks you hung the moon. The way she looks at you…if that isn't a look of love, I don't know what is."

Braden grinned. He felt a bit sappy, but Beulah's words served as encouragement. He didn't know how he was going to express his feelings to Piper, but he was intent on doing it as soon as they could share a private moment.

If Beulah was right, Piper would be receptive to what he had to tell her, and they could move forward together. He'd made one big decision this morning. In order to start fresh in Owl Creek, he needed to come clean with Piper. And it terrified him because he knew in doing so, he might kill any chance they had of a future together.

Piper looked around the crowded diner with a feeling of contentment. Business had been steadily increasing over the past few weeks due to the holiday stroll and the countdown to Christmas events. She couldn't even guess the number of milkshakes they'd served or the specialty pie orders that had been placed since they'd added them to the menu. Things had gotten so crazy with the pies that they'd been forced to set up a separate baking location at Birdie's house to complete the orders. It seemed everyone wanted to take home a holiday pie for Christmas.

Thank you, Lord. She felt blessed beyond measure. Her faith in the Snowy Owl's future had been restored. For so long Piper had been living in fear. At the moment she was hopeful for a new chapter at the diner. She no longer had to walk around on eggshells waiting for the bottom to fall out. Now she felt as if she could truly enjoy Christmas without fearing what was coming down the road. She still had a lot of work to do in order to keep the diner in good financial straits, but if business continued at this pace and if Pie in the Sky was successful, her establishment would be secure.

God was good! He had shepherded her through the storm and brought Braden back to Owl Creek where he belonged. It was beginning to look like a very merry Christmas indeed. What had sparked between herself and Braden was exciting and full of promise. Thinking of him in a romantic light was new to her. It still felt surprising to her that their friendship was morphing into something else. Perhaps she'd always had a little bit of a crush on him.

Hadn't her mother always told her that the best relationships started off as friendships? Braden was trustworthy and kind, as well as being extremely easy on the eyes and humorous. If she had to make a list of attributes a romantic partner should possess, Braden would check off all the boxes. Lately she'd had a serious case of the butterflies every time he was around. It was scary to even acknowledge it to herself, but she was in love with her best friend.

Although she'd had crushes before and dated a little bit, Piper had never in her life felt anything remotely like what she felt for Braden.

"What has you smiling like that?" Clara asked as she popped into the kitchen to check in with her regarding the lunch menu. "You look as if you just won the lottery."

"Can't a girl be happy? Christmas is coming, Clara. The most wonderful time of the year," she said in a singsong voice. For good measure, Piper spread her arms wide in dramatic fashion.

Clara looked at her skeptically. "Whatever you say, boss."

Piper headed back out to the dining room. She loved seeing all the familiar faces settling in for a good meal. This was her favorite part of owning the Snowy Owl. The people were at the heart of it all. For the next hour, Piper busied herself on the floor, helping seat customers, taking orders and cleaning up the counter area.

"Hi, Piper. I just wanted to come over and say hello before I leave." The deep voice quickly brought her out of her thoughts. Tim Carroll, the tall, handsome man who had just approached her at the counter had always had a boyish charm. He'd been in the same class as Piper throughout their childhood and teen years. He was one of Braden's buddies.

"Hey, Tim. Long time no see. How have you been?" Piper asked, feeling nostalgic at the sight of him. As small children they'd chased each other around the playground and attended each other's birthday parties. It had been way too long since she'd seen Tim.

"Pretty good, Piper. I can't complain. I've been living in Homer for the past few years. I came back to visit my parents for the holidays."

"Aww. They must be happy to see you back." Christmas was a time for family and togetherness and festivity. And this year, it heralded new beginnings for both the diner and her relationship with Braden.

"I've thought about you and your family a lot since that day on the trails."

"Thanks for saying so. We're holding up as well

as we can. The holidays are tough. But this year I'm trying to focus on our blessings and carrying on daddy's legacy with the diner."

"You're doing a great job. Everyone is raving about the new additions to the menu. The Oreo milkshake is my favorite." Tim patted his stomach. "Jack would be so proud of you." He made a face. "I was snowmobiling that afternoon with Braden. I know how broken up he was about Jack's death. One moment they were arguing and the next Braden was heroically giving him CPR."

Piper frowned. What was Tim talking about? She bristled against the suggestion. He had to be mistaken. "Arguing? No. You must be thinking of someone else." Suddenly, she felt flustered. Why would he say something like that about Braden and her father? It made no sense.

A look of confusion crossed over his face. "No. I was there. I heard the whole thing. I'm sure it would have blown over later, but unfortunately the crash happened. I—I'm sorry. I shouldn't have brought it up."

"Well now that you have, what was the argument about?" she asked. She needed to know the details. Her father and Braden had always gotten along so well. What could have happened that day to change things?

"Piper, I shouldn't have mentioned it." Tim's face appeared ashen.

"But you did," she said. "Tell me." Her sharp tone brooked no argument.

Tim hesitated before answering. Seconds ticked

by before he said, "Jack confronted Braden about racing fast on the trails. He said there had been some complaints. They had a little back and forth before Jack took off down the trail."

Disbelief washed over her. "This can't be true. Braden would have told me."

Tim shook his head. "I've upset you. I really didn't mean to do that. I should have kept my mouth shut," he muttered. Tim sent her a sorrowful look before darting away.

Piper grabbed hold of the counter to steady herself. Tim's disclosure regarding Braden's argument with her father left her feeling stunned. It just didn't gel with everything Braden had told her about that tragic afternoon. They'd talked countless times about the day of the accident without Braden ever disclosing that he had argued with her father. Why would Braden have lied to her? There was no disputing the authenticity of Tim's account. He'd always been a truthful person, and he had nothing to gain by making up a story about Braden. She put her head in her hands. Her temples began to throb, and a sickening sensation washed over her. Was this the reason Braden had been so disconnected with her since his return?

Suddenly it felt as if she had complete and utter clarity. This was what had been standing between them for the last few years. This was the reason why he hadn't been himself around her. She let out a sob. Braden had fought with her father before he crashed his snowmobile, which meant her dad had been upset before the accident. Had their fight distracted Jack? So many questions were racing through her mind. Had he been responsible for her father's death?

"Are you all right?" Jorge had walked up to her without her even realizing it. He was peering at her with a look of concern stamped on his face.

"I just need a minute," she said, heading back toward the kitchen and grabbing her parka so she could slip out through the back door. Her ears were ringing, and she could barely focus. Clara called out to her, but Piper kept walking, intent on leaving the diner before she broke down in front of everyone. A cold blast of wintry air hit her squarely in the face as she pushed the door open. Her eyes burned from a mixture of the fierce wind and her utter devastation. She pressed her eyes closed and began to pray. *Please, Lord. Don't let this be true.*

"Piper! Clara told me you were out here. What's going on?" The sound of Braden's voice echoed like a gunshot.

No! She didn't want to face him right now. Her emotions were all over the place. She needed time to process what she'd just learned before she spoke with Braden.

"Talk to me, Piper!" There was an urgency in Braden's tone she couldn't ignore.

Piper slowly turned to face him. Tears slid down her face, but she didn't bother wiping them away. She knew with a deep certainty that more would be coming. It felt as if her heart had been ripped out of her chest. Anger bubbled up inside her with such a ferocity it frightened her. She'd known for a long time something was off with Braden, but she'd let her guard down because she'd been falling for him. He'd made her feel things she now felt ashamed of.

"It's freezing out here. Come back inside and tell me what happened," Braden suggested. His features were furrowed with worry. Any other time she would have found it endearing. At the moment it only served to intensify her rage.

"What happened?" she asked, glaring at him. She strode toward him, swallowing up the distance between them in a few angry strides. "I'll tell you what happened! I just found out that my best friend has been lying to me for four years about the circumstances of my father's death."

The moment Braden saw Piper's face he knew with a deep certainty that he was wading into dangerous waters. The expression stamped on his best friend's face was one of betrayal and utter devastation. Regret speared through his chest. Why hadn't he summoned the courage to tell her the truth when he had the chance? Now she would never believe he'd been planning to tell her the news this afternoon.

Words failed him. What could he say? That he'd been a coward? That he'd failed to do what was right from the very beginning? More than anything, he wanted to express his regret and to let her know how deeply he cared about her. She was everything to him. Losing her was unfathomable.

Lord, please give me strength to face my truths

*and acknowledge my weakness. Show me the path
to make things right with Piper.*

"I'm not exactly sure what you've heard, but I
haven't been completely honest with you about the
day Jack died. We had an argument before we set
off on our snowmobiles. He was upset with me and
some friends about some reports he'd heard."

"Why didn't you tell me?" she asked in a raspy
voice. "How could you keep something like that from
me for all this time?"

"Because I didn't want to lose you. It sounds pa-
thetic, but it's true. It's the reason I left Owl Creek."
He let out an agonized sound. "I felt like the worst
person in the world comforting you after he died.
You leaned on me, and I wanted more than anything
to shoulder you through your grief. After a while I
couldn't bear to look you in the eye, all the while
knowing what I was keeping from you."

"You stood by me while I grieved, then six months
later you left town." She put her head in her hands
and let out a groan. "You leaving Owl Creek hurt me
so much. In the space of a few months, I lost both
of my anchors."

"It was eating me up inside, knowing if I told you
about the disagreement I had with your father you
might blame me for the crash," he admitted. "I'm
so sorry, Piper."

"So he was agitated before he hit the trails? Is
that what you're saying?" she asked, angrily wiping
away tears from her cheeks.

Braden nodded. "Yes. He was furious when he came looking for me and we went back and forth."

"And what did you say to him?"

"I—I asked him why he was focusing on me. I pushed back against his allegations because they weren't true. He told me I was being prideful."

Piper's brown eyes went wide with shock. "That doesn't even sound like him. He must have been really angry to say those things and to confront you."

"He was pretty upset. I'd never had a cross word with him in my entire life. He just seemed annoyed from the moment he approached me. It escalated from there."

Piper flinched as if he'd struck her. "So he went snowmobiling after this awful fight?"

"Yes. The way we left things wasn't good, but I promise you, we would have mended things if he—"

"Hadn't been killed?" Piper's tone was as emotionless as her expression. It felt as if Piper had thrown a grenade down on the ground and it had exploded in his face. There was nothing he could say to dispute her father's heartbreaking death. In her eyes that made him guilty. He could see it emanating from her eyes.

He nodded. "Yes. In a million years I don't think either one of us ever imagined those would be the last words we ever exchanged. And I'm more regretful about it than anything else in my life. I loved Jack, Piper. I considered him a friend."

Piper's lips were trembling. "Then why didn't you tell the truth? Or didn't you think it mattered?"

"Of course it matters. I was afraid of losing you. That's my only defense." He shrugged. "It may sound as if I acted terribly, but it deeply affected my life. I left town and everyone I love because of it. It was never something I forgot about. It's been with me this whole time."

She shook her head fiercely. "I still don't understand why you didn't tell me the day of the crash. That's not how you treat someone you care about!"

"You know how much I care about you. Working together has been amazing. And we've become so much more than friends." Braden reached out to grasp her hand.

She recoiled from his touch. "I can't trust you. You lied to me for years about my father's final moments. What you did was cruel and self-serving. You kissed me, all the while knowing you were harboring this terrible secret." She ran a shaky hand through her hair. "You told me he was happy before the crash and that's not true. That gave me so much comfort, and now I know it was nothing more than a fabrication to cover up what really happened."

He reached out and lightly grabbed her by the shoulders, forcing her to look him in the eye. "No, Piper. That's not true. He *was* happy and joyful before we argued. Everything I told you was true." He winced. "I left out the part about our argument, which was incredibly wrong and foolish of me. I've blamed myself for Jack's death for a long time, but in the end, I think it was just an accident. A terrible, heart-wrenching accident."

Piper glared at him. "One that forever altered my life…and caused my family unbearable pain. It wasn't just an accident to us. It was a bomb that went off and destroyed our family. We lost our very foundation. We were ripped apart at the seams."

"I—I didn't mean it like that," he said, wishing he wasn't so clumsy with his words. He'd inadvertently made it sound as if Jack's death was insignificant when in reality it had been catastrophic to all those who loved him. He couldn't even begin to put into words how deeply it had affected him. He'd been broken in the aftermath of Jack's death. And to this day, he still wondered if Jack crashing his snowmobile had been his fault.

Piper ducked her head. She wrapped her arms around her middle and began to rock back slightly. She looked as if she was in a different world, far away from his reach.

"Piper, don't shut down on me. What's been blossoming between us has been incredible. I know you feel it too."

"Anything I've felt for you makes me ashamed now." He reached out to touch her, but she took a step backward. "Go away, Braden! I can't stand to look at you. You don't belong here."

"Please, don't say that. I know you're angry, but we can talk this out. I can fix this." He heard the pleading tone in his own voice.

"There's nothing to fix, Braden. Nothing at all. And there never will be!" Piper took one last look at him before turning away from him and heading back into the Snowy Owl. Her angry strides mirrored everything she'd just said to him. He knew he would just be wasting his time to ask for mercy. She was done with him.

He deserved every single bit of her censure and disdain. Everything had blown up in his face just as he'd decided to tell Piper his secret. Timing was everything in life. If only he'd had the courage to speak up earlier. Perhaps he could have salvaged their friendship.

The verse from Luke had been echoing through his mind for weeks now. "For nothing is secret, that shall not be made manifest; neither any thing hid, that shall not be known and come abroad." His truths had come to light, and now, just as he had feared for the last four years, he'd lost Piper. And somehow it felt way worse than in his darkest imaginings.

He had no idea how to move forward without her in his life. She was the sun everything revolved around. Piper was the one who knew him best—warts and all. Their friendship had always been special to him, but now he felt so much more. Somewhere along the way he'd fallen in love with her. It was overwhelming to know his heart was wrapped up in someone so completely it no longer belonged to him. But it didn't matter because he'd lost her.

There was no doubt in his mind that Piper wanted nothing to do with him from this point forward. She'd radiated pure rage and disgust. Throughout their lives Braden had always known exactly what to do in order to make Piper come around after little squabbles and arguments. This time felt incredibly different. It felt like a door had slammed shut on him, one he had no way of ever opening up again.

Chapter Twelve

The last few days had been pure torture for Piper. She couldn't stop thinking about Braden, even though she was still convinced that she never wanted to lay eyes on him again. It was a horrific realization to know she'd lost so much in one fell swoop. She would never get over this rift between the two of them. Her life wouldn't be the same without her best friend in it.

She looked around the diner and took a steadying breath. She really needed to keep it together and remember what she'd been fighting for this whole time. This evening was the grand debut of Pie in the Sky, and she needed the celebration to go off without a hitch. Not having Braden at her side would be a painful reminder of all that had transpired between them. Piper wasn't sure the ache would ever go away, but she needed to put one foot in front of the other and keep the focus on increasing profit.

Thankfully, Jorge was back at work, and along with Otis, Birdie, Clara and her regular wait staff, they would be ready to show off the pies tonight. The Snowy Owl would be open for regular dining, but they would be celebrating her new venture and heavily promoting the pies.

Thanks to Elena, everything in the diner looked festive. She'd placed balloons all over the establishment, along with a few fun signs. Everything matched up with their Christmas decor. Birdie had placed colorful ribbons on each of the pie boxes, giving the baked goods a celebratory look. Piper stood back and surveyed the row of pies she'd placed on the counter. Despite the situation with Braden, she couldn't help but feel excited.

Her mother, who'd agreed to help out tonight, joined her at the counter. "Where's Braden? He was the one who encouraged you to focus on pies in the first place. I thought he'd be the first one through the doors."

Piper winced at the mention of his name. She was trying so hard to push him out of her heart and mind. "He won't be coming around anymore," she answered quietly. She didn't want everyone to hear the news. The last thing she needed was to be the subject of town gossip. She took her mother's hand and led her through the kitchen into the back office.

Once they were inside the small room, Trudy immediately began to pepper her daughter with questions.

"What's going on? Did the two of you have a fight?" Trudy asked. Alarm rang out in her voice.

"It wasn't a fight," Piper said, letting out a sigh. "He's been keeping a huge secret from me, and I found out that he's nothing more than a big, fat liar."

"Piper! You don't mean that!" Trudy admonished her. "He's your oldest and dearest friend in the world. You shouldn't speak about him like that."

Her cheeks felt heated as a result of Trudy's sharp rebuke. Ever since she was a small child, she'd hated being the object of her mother's wrath. Braden deserved every ounce of her scorn. Her mother needed to realize that she wasn't being unreasonable.

"Mama, I do mean it," she said, her lips quivering. "He lied to me. Ever since Daddy's accident, Braden has been withholding the truth from all of us!"

Trudy gasped. "Whatever do you mean?"

Tears welled in her eyes. Just when she thought there were no more tears to shed, more materialized. Her pain felt almost unbearable. "That day on the mountain, Braden and Daddy had a big argument. Daddy was angry with him about some rumors he'd heard about Braden being reckless on the trails."

Trudy frowned. "That doesn't sound like Braden at all. He's always been so responsible. And caring."

"Well, it's true. They had a terrible argument. As a result, Daddy was upset. He went out on the trails after their fight, which Braden conveniently left out of his narrative. He took credit for doing CPR and trying to save Daddy's life, but the truth is he's responsible for what happened."

"I don't think you can put this on Braden," her mother said with a shake of her head. "I've known him all of your life. There's no way I'll ever believe he was so ugly to Jack that it led to the crash." She reached out and squeezed Piper's hand.

"It's all his fault!" Piper said, shaking her head.

Trudy's gaze hardened. "How do you figure that?"

Piper frowned at her mother. "Didn't you hear me? Daddy called Braden out about driving irresponsibly, and instead of just apologizing, Braden fought back and it led to a heated argument. Daddy wasn't in the right frame of mind to go snowmobiling, which led to the accident. You know how much he took things to heart. It probably broke his spirit."

"Oh, my darling. It's not that simple." Trudy sat down in a chair, shoulders slumped. "Have you been looking all this time to blame someone? If that's true, you're going to have to start with me."

Piper sat down across from her mother. "What are you talking about? You're not at fault for anything."

Trudy folded her hands in front of her and heaved a tremendous sigh. "The morning of the accident your father and I had a spat. I didn't want him to go snowmobiling because there were a hundred little things to fix around the inn. The water heater was acting up, and one of the dining room table legs was wobbly. Not to mention a bunch of other stuff that seems so unimportant now. It struck me as selfish of him to go joy riding while the place was falling apart around us. I told him he was being childish, and he stormed off." She blinked back tears. "You have no idea how much I wish I'd been kinder and gentler that day. Over the past four years, I've had to live with the fact that the love story we shared wasn't on full display on the last day of his life."

"Oh, Mama. I'm so sorry! You and Daddy loved each other so much."

"We did," Trudy acknowledged, dabbing at her eyes with a tissue. "When I lost Hank's father, it felt like my heart shriveled up into nothing. I promised myself I'd never love again. Then one day, Jack came barreling into my life with his magnetic smile and wide open heart. I fell faster than a ton of logs down an icy hill." She began to chuckle. "No matter what we last said to each other, our life together was a testament to the love we shared."

Piper let out a sob and jumped up from her seat, wrapping her arms tightly around her mother. "Of course it is. I've always known how fortunate I was to grow up witnessing your love story. You've truly shown me what love between a couple looks like. Neither one of you was perfect, but you loved one another wholly and completely."

Piper kissed her mother's cheek. "That will always outshine a little squabble. You lived in love every day."

"There's something else," Trudy admitted. "I probably should have mentioned it at the time, but we were all so grief stricken I couldn't even think straight. His doctor suspected Jack might have had a heart attack that day. He'd been dealing with a lot of fluctuations in his blood pressure over the past few years."

Piper felt as if someone had ripped blinders off her. She'd known about her father's high blood pressure, but a medical condition had never been linked to the accident. Now, according to her mother, it was possible he'd suffered a heart attack.

She ran a shaky hand over her face. What had she done in blaming Braden? She'd hurt him badly with her baseless accusations. She'd been mean-hearted and cruel.

"Mama. I said terrible things to him about causing Daddy's death. How can I ever face him again? I told him never to come around the diner and that I was done with him."

Trudy made a tutting sound. "Where there's love there is understanding. Compassion. Redemption. You and Braden have been joined at the hip since you were little. I may be completely off base here, but I suspect your feelings for him have blossomed into something else. Am I right?"

Her heart sank. So far she'd been keeping her feelings for Braden under wraps. Coming to terms with these budding sentiments hadn't been easy. "I-is it that obvious?" she asked, already knowing the answer.

"Probably not to most folks." Trudy reached out and tweaked Piper's nose. "But I know you inside and out, my darling. You're a lot like Jack. You wear your heart on your sleeve."

Piper let out a groan. "I don't know what to do. I need to apologize and tell him how wrong I was to blame him."

"I think that's a great start," her mother said, nodding. "And perhaps there are a few other things you should tell him while you're at it." Trudy wiggled her eyebrows. "Pour your heart out to him. Don't let a single thing remain unsaid."

She bit her lip. "I—I don't know if I'm brave enough to do all of that. I think we've both been feeling this pull in each other's direction, but it's complicated due to our long-standing friendship." Piper swallowed past the fear clogging her throat. "Ever since he took off from Owl Creek, I've been afraid of losing him."

"The only sure way of losing him is if you don't clear the air. Words left unspoken tend to lead to missed opportunities."

Her mother's words hit their mark. She was right. If only Braden had told her the truth four years ago instead of staying silent out of fear and guilt. Piper didn't want to make the same mistake. She refused to allow another day to go by without letting Braden know what he meant to her and how she forgave him for withholding the truth about the accident. "You're right. I have to try and fix things. No matter what, he'll always be my best friend." And perhaps if she was truly fortunate, something infinitely more tender.

Piper glanced at her watch. She had a few hours before the Pie in the Sky launch party was set to take place. The truth was it wouldn't really be a celebration without the one person who had made all of this possible with his vision and heart. It made her sick to her stomach that she'd judged him so harshly. *Judge not lest ye be judged.* She wasn't a perfect person, and she'd made a lot of mistakes. She'd pushed him away out of her own hurt and pain. Grief was such a long process, and she was still wading knee-deep in the loss.

Losing Braden in addition to her dad would be way more than she could bear.

Chapter Thirteen

It didn't take Piper long to track Braden down. She'd stopped at the chocolate factory where Beulah had told her where to find him—at his favorite spot at the Gray Owl mountains. It explained why he hadn't been picking up any of her calls. Cell phone reception outside of town wasn't always reliable. She had made one stop before getting on the road. It had been important to pick something up at Trudy's inn. As she drove nearby the area where Otis lived, she couldn't help but think of her father and the accident. This area was so pristine and beautiful, yet she'd stayed away from it due to all of the painful memories related to her father's death.

Four years was a long time to stay away from a place she truly loved. As of right now she was no longer going to avoid this precious land. All of her life her parents had taught her to cherish her Alaskan heritage and to embrace all it had to offer.

Her heart skipped a beat at the sight of Braden. He

was standing with a snowboard in his hand, cheeks reddened from the cold, body poised for action. This was Braden at his core. *Her* Braden. An adventurer. An outdoorsman. It was who he was, in addition to being an incredibly loyal friend and the man she loved beyond measure. She could only hope he felt a fraction of what she held in her heart for him. Come what may, she would soon find out.

Now that she was within a few feet of him she didn't know what to say. Her words were stuck in her throat. If she said what was weighing on her heart, there would be no turning back. It was so hard to be vulnerable without knowing if she would be accepted or rejected.

"Braden!" She called out to him, drawing his attention away from his next run. He whirled around at the sound of her voice.

"Piper. What are you doing here?" A look of confusion was stamped on his face. "You're the last person I expected to see."

"I'd almost forgotten how beautiful it is up here," she said, her eyes darting all around her. The very air she was breathing seemed different. Cleaner. Purer. It felt like a completely different world from in town.

"It is, but I know you didn't trek all the way here to tell me that." He was looking at her warily as if expecting her to unload on him again. Frankly, she couldn't really blame him. Her words had been brutal.

"Do you remember that time you put the bullfrog in my lunch box when we were in second grade?" she asked.

Braden shifted from one foot to the other. "How could I forget? You didn't talk to me for a solid week. You really made me sweat it out."

"And then you came over to my house and told me how sorry you were. You gave me a box and inside was your favorite set of Lego pieces. I knew right then and there how remorseful you truly were."

Braden scoffed. He placed his palm on his chest. "It was a painful sacrifice for the best friend I've ever had." His voice lowered. "Or ever will have."

She ducked her head for a moment to compose herself. It was important to get through this without allowing emotion to completely take over. Piper stepped closer toward him, swallowing up the distance between them. She reached into her pocket and pulled out a box. Time had been of the essence so she hadn't been able to put a pretty ribbon on it. It was no-frills. "Braden, I'm so sorry for all the terrible things I said to you. It's no excuse, but I think I've been looking to blame someone or something for what happened to my dad. It took my mom to point it out to me."

Piper held out the gift box to him. Braden dropped his snowboard and took a few steps toward her so that they were standing within inches of each other. He took it, then lightly shook it. "Do you want me to open it now? Or is this a wait until Christmas morning type of thing?"

"Now, please," she answered. The sound of her heart thumping wildly inside her chest echoed in her ears. She'd never felt such an odd sensation as this one. She wanted to throw herself in Braden's arms and run away at the same time. So much was riding on his reaction to her gift.

She watched as Braden opened the box and pulled out the stuffed red heart. It had a few years of wear and tear on it, but it was one of the most treasured items she owned. Her grandmother had given it to her many years ago, and as Braden well knew, it was a priceless keepsake.

Braden swung his gaze up and locked eyes with her. "Are you giving this to me?"

"Yes," she said with a nod. "I'm not only giving you something that's precious to me, but I'm giving you my heart—the one that's beating so fast right now in my chest."

"Please don't tell me you mean just as a friend." He appeared to be holding his breath waiting for her answer.

Piper let out a shaky laugh. "You'll always be my best friend, but my feelings for you go well beyond that. I'm in love with you, Braden North."

Braden reached out and clasped her mittened hand in his. "Say it again, Piper. I want to make sure I'm not imagining things."

"I love you," she said, feeling breathless as she said the words once again. It was a freeing sensation to acknowledge the love she held in her heart for Braden.

"I love you back," he said, letting out a deeply held breath. "I think I've loved you for most of my life, but I didn't even realize it until recently. All I know is that my life is better with you in it."

"I'm glad you feel that way even though I was so tough on you the other day." She wrinkled her nose. "I'm really ashamed for lashing out at you in that manner."

He ran his hand across her cheek. "I should have told you the truth right from the beginning. I was just so afraid of losing you it messed with my head. I've been racked with guilt ever since the accident."

"I don't blame you and I forgive you for not telling me the truth. There are so many things that may have contributed to the crash. I wish you'd been honest with me about it a long time ago. That way we could have worked through it together. You'll never lose me. You're imprinted on my heart, Braden." Her throat felt tight, but at this moment it was a result of overwhelming happiness.

"Like you're etched on mine," he answered, his face lit up like Christmas morning.

Piper stood on her tippy toes and pressed a tender kiss on Braden's lips. Joy washed over her as he kissed her back enthusiastically. As they broke apart, they stared into each other's eyes without speaking, both content to savor the special moment. She no longer had to worry about anything standing in the way of their relationship. Everything had come to light, and they were no longer in the shadows.

"I've been reminded lately about not living with a spirit of fear, but of power and love," he said, breaking the silence. "That's how I want to live my life."

"Me too. I'm so incredibly blessed to be surrounded by love."

She took a deep breath. "I loved my dad so much and I still miss him like crazy, especially during the holidays. He made everything so special for all of us."

Braden ran his hand over the top of her head, down past her curly mane. "He loved you, Piper. And he was so incredibly proud of you. Your family was everything to him."

"I know he'd be tickled about the pies and the milkshakes. It really helps to think of him with a big smile on his face and giving me a huge thumbs-up."

"I can see it. And what I told you was true. Jack was joyful before he died. I saw him whipping around the trails as if he was flying on a cloud." Braden grinned. Piper could tell he was now remembering that day with more nuances than simply through a lens of guilt. They had both turned a corner, which would allow them to move forward with their lives. Together.

"There's so much to be thankful for this Christmas. I'm really blessed to have you in my life, and things are steadily improving at the diner. I don't think that I even dared to dream everything would come together like this."

"Some things are just meant to be." Braden dipped his head down and kissed her temple.

"Speaking of gratitude, we really need to get back to the Snowy Owl. The pie launch is in less than an hour. The rest of the team is holding down the fort for us."

"Us? Does that mean you want me to tag along?"

"Braden! There wouldn't be a pie launch without you. You came up with the idea of selling pies in the first place." She looked up at him. "I'd feel honored if you'd stand by my side as we officially launch Pie in the Sky to Owl Creek."

"I'd love to stand by your side. It seems fitting since I'm going to invest in Pie in the Sky."

Piper's jaw dropped. "Wh-what? Are you serious?"

Braden dipped his head down and kissed her. "I've never been more serious about anything in my life. I'm not employed at the moment, so I'd be honored to become your silent partner in the pie business. I believe in you."

"I believe in us," she whispered, gazing up at him with pure happiness and joy. They were getting the happy ending she hadn't even thought was possible. Their friendship had turned into a love she knew would last a lifetime.

Epilogue

One year later

It was a beautiful December morning in Owl Creek, Piper realized as she walked hand in hand with Braden along the wooded trail, Rudy trailing closely behind. The temperature had plummeted overnight to a chilly 20 degrees Fahrenheit, but Piper couldn't have felt any happier. Spending time with Braden always gave her joy.

"I still feel a little bit guilty taking the afternoon off from the diner," Piper confessed. A storm had been forecast for later that day, as evidenced by the cloudy sky and the snow swirling from the sky. They still had a few hours before it hit Owl Creek full force, and they were making the most of the great Alaskan outdoors.

"Are you kidding me? After all the hard work you've put in to turn things around at the Snowy

Owl, you deserve a little fun." He squeezed her hand. "Have I told you lately how proud of you I am?"

Piper looked over at him and grinned. "You have, but I'll never get tired of hearing it. If it wasn't for you, I'm not sure I ever would have gotten Pie in the Sky off the ground. I'd still be struggling to find a way out of a very dicey financial situation."

"It was all you, Piper. You're the one who makes the most delicious pies in all of Alaska." He let out a chuckle. "Maybe even in the entire United States."

She reached out and swept her mittened hand across his cheek. "You believed in me, Braden, and I'll never forget it. Because of you I managed to save the diner from financial ruin."

Braden stopped in his tracks and turned toward her. "Of course I had faith in you. You can do anything you set your mind to accomplish. I love you, Piper."

"I love you too, Braden. I'm so happy there's nothing standing between us any longer." She reached up on her tippy toes and placed a tender kiss on his lips. She clung to the front of his parka and pulled him closer toward her. She let out a sigh as the kiss ended, feeling more content than she'd ever imagined. Being with Braden was the culmination of a lifetime of friendship and camaraderie. It was a wonder it had taken both of them so long to see what was right under their noses. But God had given them both a little nudge in the right direction.

"You're not only my best friend, Piper, but you're the person I want to walk through life with by my side. You encouraged me to open up my company specializing in Alaskan adventures. I don't know if I would have taken that step if it hadn't been for you." Braden took a deep breath and began to dig around in his jacket pocket. After a few moments of fumbling, he pulled out a cedar box and propped it open, revealing a brilliant diamond ring. "I want to take so many more steps with you."

Piper let out a shocked sound. "Braden!" she exclaimed as she laid eyes on the heart-shaped diamond sparkling and shimmering at her from inside the box.

Braden smiled at her tenderly. "I feel like this is the most natural thing in the world. It couldn't have ever been anyone but you. You've had my heart since we were kids. I just didn't know it until recently. It's like I finally had all the pieces to the puzzle once I realized I was head over heels in love with you."

Tears were streaming down Piper's face and she didn't bother wiping them away. She was too busy listening intently to Braden's words. It was as if her heart had been awaiting this moment for her entire life. She didn't want to miss a moment of it.

"Piper, will you spend the rest of your life with me? Will you be my best friend for the rest of our days?" Braden asked, his voice cracking with emotion. Although he was nervous about proposing, this moment felt more real than anything else ever had. Marrying Piper would feel like coming home. *If* she said yes.

Piper laughed and grinned, her joy overflowing. "Of course I will. I love you so much, Braden. I always have. I always will."

"You're going to have to take off those mittens so I can put this ring on your finger," Braden said, plucking the diamond from its throne and holding it up as Piper quickly removed the mitten from her left hand. Braden slid the ring on her finger and lowered his head down to place a celebratory kiss on Piper's lips.

When the kiss ended, Piper said, "I feel so blessed. Our deep, abiding friendship led to love."

Braden nodded. "And to a lifetime of adventures. Owl Creek will always be our home base, but there's a big world out there I want to explore with you."

Piper held her hand up and admired her engagement ring. "I can't wait to travel with you now that the Snowy Owl is doing better. I know it will be in good hands with Jorge if we spend time away from Alaska. It's amazing how everything can turn around in a heartbeat."

"You just have to believe, my love," Braden said, pressing a kiss against her temple.

"Oh, I believe, Braden. And I always will."

* * * * *

If you enjoyed this story,
look for the other Owl Creek books
by Belle Calhoune:

Dear Reader,

Thank you for joining me on this heartwarming Alaskan journey. It was a lot of fun writing a love story featuring two people who were lifelong friends until love took them by surprise. I hope you enjoyed Piper and Braden's story. They truly deserved their happily-ever-after. Piper and Braden share a wonderful friendship that goes all the way back to the cradle. Their lives have always been entwined.

Braden has a lot of guilt about his role in Jack's accident, which gets in the way of his relationship with Piper since he's keeping secrets. Piper in turn hasn't fully dealt with the loss of her father and is still grieving the tragedy.

Family is a huge component in all of my stories. Both Piper and Braden belong to loving, wonderful families who provide support and endless amounts of love. That's so very important in life—to feel supported and accepted.

As always, writing for the Love Inspired line is an honor. Being able to work in my pajamas is a huge perk of being an author. I love hearing from readers, however you choose to reach out to me. I can be found on my Author Belle Calhoune Facebook page or at bellecalhoune.com.

Blessings,
Belle

**WE HOPE YOU ENJOYED
THIS BOOK FROM**

LOVE INSPIRED

INSPIRATIONAL ROMANCE

Uplifting stories of faith, forgiveness and hope.

Fall in love with stories where faith helps
guide you through life's challenges, and discover
the promise of a new beginning.

6 NEW BOOKS AVAILABLE EVERY MONTH!

LIHALO2020

COMING NEXT MONTH FROM
Love Inspired

Available October 20, 2020

A HAVEN FOR CHRISTMAS
North Country Amish • by Patricia Davids
After an accident lands Tully Lange on widow Becca Beachy's farm, she's determined to show the troubled *Englischer* a true Amish Christmas. But even as she falls for him, Becca knows anything between them is forbidden. Will she have to let him go, or is there hope for a future?

AN AMISH HOLIDAY FAMILY
Green Mountain Blessings • by Jo Ann Brown
When Mennonite midwife Beth Ann Overholt went to Evergreen Corners to help rebuild after a flood, she never expected to take in three abandoned children—especially with an Amish bachelor by her side. But this temporary family with Robert Yoder might just turn out to be the perfect Christmas gift...

THE RANCHER'S HOLIDAY ARRANGEMENT
Mercy Ranch • by Brenda Minton
With his family in town for Christmas pressuring him to move back home and join their business, foreman Joe Lawson will do anything to stay on Mercy Ranch—even pretend Daisy West is his fiancée. But can he protect his heart from his boss's prodigal daughter and her adorable foster twins?

HIS CHRISTMAS WISH
Wander Canyon • by Allie Pleiter
Still reeling from his sister's death, Jake Sanders intends to give his orphaned nephew the best Christmas ever. So when little Cole's preschool teacher, Emma Mullins, offers to help him care for the boy, he's grateful for her guidance. But can their blossoming love survive the dark truth Emma's hiding?

THE CHRISTMAS BARGAIN
by Lisa Carter
Unwilling to attend a wedding alone, art teacher Lila Penry makes a deal with Sam Gibson: she'll give his niece private lessons if he'll be her date. But now with the town convinced they're an item just as Lila accepts an out-of-state dream job, local matchmakers won't stop until these two find their happily-ever-after.

SURPRISE CHRISTMAS FAMILY
Thunder Ridge • by Renee Ryan
Armed with custody papers, Hope Jeffries heads to a small Colorado town to convince her nieces' father to give her full guardianship. But Walker Evans is the wrong twin—the girls' uncle. As they track down his brother, can Walker and Hope join forces to give their little nieces a traditional family Christmas?

LOOK FOR THESE AND OTHER LOVE INSPIRED BOOKS WHEREVER BOOKS ARE SOLD, INCLUDING MOST BOOKSTORES, SUPERMARKETS, DISCOUNT STORES AND DRUGSTORES.

LICNM1020

SPECIAL EXCERPT FROM

LOVE INSPIRED
INSPIRATIONAL ROMANCE

*When Mennonite midwife Beth Ann Overholt went to
Evergreen Corners to help rebuild after a flood, she
never expected to take in three abandoned children—
especially with an Amish bachelor by her side. But this
temporary family with Robert Yoder might just turn out
to be the perfect Christmas gift...*

Read on for a sneak preview of
An Amish Holiday Family
by Jo Ann Brown,
available November 2020 from Love Inspired!

"You don't ever complain. You take care of someone
else's *kinder* without hesitation, and you're giving them a
home they haven't had in who knows how long."

"Trust me. There was plenty of hesitation on my part."

"I do trust you."

Beth Ann's breath caught at the undercurrent of
emotion in his simple answer. "I'm glad to hear that. I got
a message from their social worker this afternoon. She
was supposed to come tomorrow, which is why I stayed
home today to make sure everything was as perfect as
possible before her visit."

"I wondered why you didn't come to the project house
today."

"That's why, but now her visit is going to be the day after tomorrow. What if she decides to take the children and place them in other homes? What if they can't be together?"

Robert paused and faced her. "Why are you looking for trouble? God brought you to the *kinder*. He knows what lies before them and before you. Trust *Him*."

"I try to." She gave him a wry grin. "It's just…just…"

"They've become important to you?"

She nodded, not trusting her voice to speak. The idea of the three youngsters being separated in the foster care system frightened her, because she wasn't sure what they might do to get back together.

"Don't forget," Robert murmured, "as important as they are to you, they're even more important to God." His smile returned. "How about getting some Christmas pie before we have to fish three *kinder* out of the brook?"

With a yelp, she rushed forward to keep Crystal from hoisting Tommy to see over the rail. Robert was right. She needed to enjoy the children while she could.

Don't miss
An Amish Holiday Family *by Jo Ann Brown,*
available November 2020 wherever
Love Inspired books and ebooks are sold.

LoveInspired.com

Copyright © 2020 by Jo Ann Ferguson

LIEXP1020

Get 4 FREE REWARDS!

We'll send you 2 FREE Books plus 2 FREE Mystery Gifts.

Love Inspired books feature uplifting stories where faith helps guide you through life's challenges and discover the promise of a new beginning.

FREE Value Over **$20**

YES! Please send me 2 FREE Love Inspired Romance novels and my 2 FREE mystery gifts (gifts are worth about $10 retail). After receiving them, if I don't wish to receive any more books, I can return the shipping statement marked "cancel." If I don't cancel, I will receive 6 brand-new novels each month and be billed just $5.24 each for the regular-print edition or $5.99 each for the larger-print edition in the U.S., or $5.74 each for the regular-print edition or $6.24 each for the larger-print edition in Canada. That's a savings of at least 13% off the cover price. It's quite a bargain! Shipping and handling is just 50¢ per book in the U.S. and $1.25 per book in Canada.* I understand that accepting the 2 free books and gifts places me under no obligation to buy anything. I can always return a shipment and cancel at any time. The free books and gifts are mine to keep no matter what I decide.

Choose one: ☐ **Love Inspired Romance Regular-Print** (105/305 IDN GNWC)   ☐ **Love Inspired Romance Larger-Print** (122/322 IDN GNWC)

Name (please print)

Address   Apt. #

City   State/Province   Zip/Postal Code

Email: Please check this box ☐ if you would like to receive newsletters and promotional emails from Harlequin Enterprises ULC and its affiliates. You can unsubscribe anytime.

Mail to the **Reader Service:**
IN U.S.A.: P.O. Box 1341, Buffalo, NY 14240-8531
IN CANADA: P.O. Box 603, Fort Erie, Ontario L2A 5X3

Want to try 2 free books from another series? Call 1-800-873-8635 or visit www.ReaderService.com.

*Terms and prices subject to change without notice. Prices do not include sales taxes, which will be charged (if applicable) based on your state or country of residence. Canadian residents will be charged applicable taxes. Offer not valid in Quebec. This offer is limited to one order per household. Books received may not be as shown. Not valid for current subscribers to Love Inspired Romance books. All orders subject to approval. Credit or debit balances in a customer's account(s) may be offset by any other outstanding balance owed by or to the customer. Please allow 4 to 6 weeks for delivery. Offer available while quantities last.

Your Privacy—Your information is being collected by Harlequin Enterprises ULC, operating as Reader Service. For a complete summary of the information we collect, how we use this information and to whom it is disclosed, please visit our privacy notice located at corporate.harlequin.com/privacy-notice. From time to time we may also exchange your personal information with reputable third parties. If you wish to opt out of this sharing of your personal information, please visit readerservice.com/consumerchoice or call 1-800-873-8635. **Notice to California Residents**—Under California law, you have specific rights to control and access your data. For more information on these rights and how to exercise them, visit corporate.harlequin.com/california-privacy.   LI20R2

LOVE INSPIRED

INSPIRATIONAL ROMANCE

IS LOOKING FOR NEW AUTHORS!

Do you have an idea for an inspirational
contemporary romance book?

Do you enjoy writing faith-based romances about small-town
men and women who overcome challenges and fall in love?

We're looking for new authors for Love Inspired,
and we want to see your story!

Check out our writing guidelines and
submit your Love Inspired manuscript at
Harlequin.com/Submit

CONNECT WITH US AT:

www.LoveInspired.com

Facebook.com/LoveInspiredBooks

Twitter.com/LoveInspiredBks

Facebook.com/groups/HarlequinConnection

LIAUTHORSBPA0820R

LOVE INSPIRED
INSPIRATIONAL ROMANCE

UPLIFTING STORIES OF FAITH, FORGIVENESS AND HOPE.

Join our social communities to connect with other readers who share your love!

Sign up for the Love Inspired newsletter at **LoveInspired.com** to be the first to find out about upcoming titles, special promotions and exclusive content.

CONNECT WITH US AT:

f Facebook.com/LoveInspiredBooks

🐦 Twitter.com/LoveInspiredBks

Facebook.com/groups/HarlequinConnection

LISOCIAL2020

HARLEQUIN

Heartfelt or suspenseful, inspiring or passionate, Harlequin has your happily-ever-after.

With new books published
every month, you are sure to find the
satisfying escape you know you deserve.

SIGN UP FOR THE HARLEQUIN NEWSLETTER

Be the first to hear about great new
reads and exciting offers!

Harlequin.com/newsletters

HNEWS2020